The Arrangement
By
Shay Gray

Published by Pink Shade Publications
Cover design by Lameka Bland and Cover Me Designs
Edited by Butterfly editorial/www.butterflyeditorial.com
Printed in the United States of America.
No part of this book may be reproduced in any form without written permission from the publisher, except by a reviewer who may quote brief passages in a review To be printed in a newspaper or magazine.

DEDICATION

To my nephew Exavier, I didn't forget you this time.

ACKNOWLEDGMENTS

I just want to say thank you to everyone that stuck by me on this journey and showed support throughout the entire process.

The biggest thanks goes to my husband, my children, my parents, my brothers, sisters, nieces, nephews, aunts, my one uncle, cousins, my very best friends, my in-law's, and countless others that are too many to name. So that no one is forgotten put your name in the space below and know that I thank you for your support.

Insert name here_____!

PROLOGUE

Terrance Davenport

I hate my life!

I'm going to jump off this building and end it right now! I'm dying! That's my real life truth!

My doctor just told me I have lung cancer. I could die today, tomorrow, or even Saturday. How is that for a checkup? A doctor shows you an x-ray, gives you a cold stare and a shoulder pat, and says:

"Sorry, ain't shit we can do. Peace."

Maybe he didn't use those exact words, but he might as well have. Up until about six months ago he would've given me a clean bill of health. I don't smoke, I don't do drugs, and I don't drink.

They say suicide is never the answer, but today it is *my* answer.

You would think, standing up here in the rain, on the ledge of my own office building wearing my new Stacy Adams, I'd think about all I have going for myself. I'd consider the people in my life: my wife, pregnant with my unborn son, *our* first child together… but not *my* first child, and my three other children.

My oldest, Nathan, is thirteen, and my two younger kids, Terrance Jr., and Teyah, are ten and two. I love them dearly, but do I want to stick around so they can watch their daddy die a slow, painful death? Hell no!

So, here I am on the ledge, staring down at the concrete pavement twenty-five feet below. I don't have any more answers. I paid for the best treatment, and followed doctor's orders, and still not a fucking thing worked.

The pain from my fists pounding my forehead is nothing compared to the pain in my heart.

Why me God?

So, I'm not a perfect man. When the wife and I are at odds, I still have sex with the mother of one of my kids. It's just to release tension. That's it. I don't love her. I love the child I have by her. I make damn good money and everyone is cared for. So how could this happen?

I got so caught up in my thoughts that I didn't notice the police cars, fire truck, ambulance, and a news van pulling up below me. I was definitely going to make the news tonight. I felt my heartbeat speed up.

What would my wife think if she could see her supposedly strong black man standing on a ledge, weak and too afraid to go on?

I was at my lowest point.

"Terrance, please step away from the ledge. We have firefighters coming up to help you back inside," a police officer shouted.

"I don't want any help. Just go, all of you please just let me do this." I heard my voice crack with emotion.

I held on and tried to steady my weight against the building. If I landed just right, I would die instantly and not have to suffer through any more pain than I was already feeling. I looked up at the clouds as the sky darkened above my head. A storm was fast approaching. I knew this before I climbed on the ledge. I figured if I waited to jump at the first clap of thunder no one would notice. Suddenly, the rain began to fall on my face mixing in with my tears.

Several minutes passed and a crowd of spectators drew near. Despite the rain I noticed some people had their cell phones out ready to post my death on YouTube and Face Book. It's a shame how social media gives people a platform to post the worse things.

I heard yelling and the sound of a door being kicked open behind me. It was the group of firefighters that had made it to my office. Surprisingly, they got past my locked office door. Now was the moment of life or death. I struggled to hold my position despite the rain making it harder for me to keep my grip. The all too familiar pain in my chest began to creep up on me.

The rain increased and the thunder boomed from the sky. It was now or never. This was my time to end it all. I could change my mind and step back inside, or I could do what I came up here to do finally. I saw the fireman's yellow jacket out the corner of my eye before my foot slipped causing me to lose my balance. Now it was too late to have any regrets, too late to change my mind. I felt like I was in a movie and someone pressed the slow motion button. Time seemed to stand still as I dropped twenty-five feet through the air. Quickly, my life flashed before my eyes and it was too late. DAMN!

Tanya Lynn Davenport

Marriage is supposed to be a beautiful union between two people who fall hopelessly in love, and decide to spend the rest of their lives together, sharing the joys and the pain, and getting through it together! Marriage is a vow you make before God to love forever until death.

So why in the hell am I sitting here pregnant and alone? Here I am supposed to be happily married to my best friend and husband of three years, pregnant with my first child, and sitting here in this doctor's office by myself, again!

That lying bastard!

My husband missed my doctor's appointment for the second time. His excuse is always that he is working, or checking on this site, or that site. Sure, being the head engineer of his own construction company is hard work, but even God took a day to rest.

Things sure aren't what they used to be. He couldn't stay out of my face when we first got together. We always traveled on vacation somewhere, or went out every Friday night trying out some new restaurant. Now we barely see each other. When we do, I am usually in the bed by ten o'clock, and he is coming in from a long day at work.

We make small talk and then it's off to dream land to start the day all over again. The days we are at home at the same time, I am downstairs watching TV, or surfing the internet, and he is in his office. This is just not what I imagined my marriage to be.

Believe me I have tried new things to get his attention. Buying new lingerie for my plus size frame, fixing my hair differently, cooking dinner with nothing but heels on, a new fragrance, makeup, different food, I have given it my all. Yet, he still shows me minor attention. The only reason I'm pregnant now is from our last vacation in St. Barth's.

Terrance was Mr. Charming there. Rubbing my feet, playing in my hair, the massages, the roses, the cards, chocolate on the pillows, candlelight dinners, and long walks on the beach I was in heaven. And then the vacation was over, and it was back to our boring married life in Chicago, Illinois.

Most people think I should be happy because Terrance provides for us very well. We have a beautiful loft apartment in the heart of downtown Chicago, I drive a brand new BMW he bought for my birthday, and the cash flow is endless due to a multi-million dollar settlement he received. I want for nothing, but the attention of my husband.

In the back of my mind I get the feeling that there is someone else, but I immediately dismiss those thoughts. He has too much drama from the two mothers of his children to add anyone new to the equation. The thought of him having kids already used to make me sick, but I loved him, so I had to accept his three children.

The more I sit here and think about it the more pissed off I find myself becoming. It's my turn to be the mother of his child, so why can't I get the attention he gave them when they were pregnant?

When I see him I'm going to kill him. I am tired of him putting me off. If I could get away with murder for reasonable doubt of his faithfulness I would do it.

The sound of my phone vibrating in my purse cut off my murderous thoughts.

"This is Tanya," I answered curtly.

"Hello is this Mrs. Terrance Davenport?"

I briefly paused at the sound of the formal voice on the other end.

"Yes."

"This is Officer Wilder from the sixth district precinct we have a bit of a situation. It seems your husband Terrance Davenport is on the ledge of an office building preparing to jump. We need you to come down to the scene immediately. Maybe, you can talk him down."

My heart stopped.

"Mrs. Davenport, are you still there?" The officer asked impatiently.

"Yes...yes I'm here. Where is he?"

"He is downtown on the corner of Chicago Avenue and La Salle Boulevard," he responded.

That's his office building. I swear this man wants to force me into an early labor. All the drama I have put up with over the years of our marriage, and now this is how he wants to end it all?

"Mrs. Davenport can we expect you in the next few minutes?" The officer was growing impatient.

"Yes sir, I'll be there."

I threw my cell phone on the seat. Tears began to cloud my eyes.

I can't believe he wants to leave me like this. This better not be over no bullshit from either one of his baby mama's either, otherwise I'll kill him myself.

I typed in the address in my GPS and floored my BMW downtown.

The drive felt like it was taking forever. I am not sure how I made it to my destination, because I felt like I was floating in mid air. In that final moment when someone's life is at the end, you think of all the arguments, everything you didn't say, everything you didn't do. Missing my doctor's appointment didn't even matter to me anymore.

I don't even remember if I said I love you this morning.

When I pulled up behind the ambulance I felt as if everything was frozen in time. My heart stopped, my body felt glued to the seat of my car, and my feet felt like heavy stones. Trying to push myself to move and get out of the car was the hardest thing to do. I was afraid. I didn't want to see Terrance like this. He was never a weak man. He was strong, confident, charismatic and in control. That was my Terrance.

This guy standing on the ledge was a stranger.

When I saw everyone looking up, I knew I was going to have to face what I didn't want to see. I pulled the hood of my rain coat over my head and shifted my eyes upward, and there he was my husband, standing in the rain, on a ledge, holding on for dear life to a piece of the building. Never in a million years would I have ever thought it would come to this.

To see him in this light I knew he had a weak point. I am not sure why, what, or who drove him to this point, but surely I couldn't just stand there and wait for him to jump to his death.

I walked over to the police officer holding the bullhorn and told him who I was. He immediately handed me the bullhorn. I took a deep breath.

My throat tightened as I tried hard to choke back the tears. I felt my son move in my belly. I'm sure he could feel my stress.

I wanted Terrance to tell me how much he hated my neon yellow raincoat I bought at a Goodwill, and to lecture me like he always did on how much money we had to buy a new one. Then we would start arguing. Although we had money, I still lived as if we could lose it all one day. "Never put your eggs in one basket," my momma would tell me, so I lived by that.

As I tried to gather my thoughts on what to say, a red Mustang pulled up throwing me off course.

I watched Terrance's baby mama, Portia; get out of the car wearing the tightest pair of jeans known to mankind, and a small top that squeezed her breasts together.

This broad did anything for attention.

Portia rolled her eyes at me as she grabbed the bullhorn from my hands. If I wasn't pregnant I would snatch her weave out of her head and toss her from the ledge of a building. So what if she had his two kids, that didn't give her the right to show her ass every time she came around.

She did everything in her power to keep some man's attention on her. Her clothes were always super tight; her makeup caked on her face, and her hair was always done in some unnaturally long weave that she created at her salon.

I knew Portia still loved Terrance, and in the back of my mind I always had this feeling he was still sleeping with her, but I didn't want to admit it.

I stood by and watched as Portia was going to try and convince Terrance to come down. If she could get him down, surely he was married to the wrong woman.

Forgetting to turn the bullhorn on she said,

"Terrance Davenport, if you don't get yo' trifling' ass off that ledge and come get your kids, I'll come push you my damn self."

The emotion was evident in her voice.

The officer grabbed the bullhorn away from her. Thank God it wasn't on. I shook my head at her utterly ridiculous performance.

"Portia why are you here? Who called you?"

She smirked before moving closer so that she was standing in my face.

"Well if it isn't the good Stepford wife, Tanya Davenport. How is my stepson doing in that belly?" She reached out her hand to rub my stomach.

I smacked her hand away.

"Don't touch me!"

Pregnant or not, I was ready to kick her ass. I was getting tired of her disrespecting me whenever she felt like it. It was time to teach her big mouth a lesson. I was happy I already had on tennis shoes, so I started taking my earrings out of my ears, until I heard someone scream.

When we both turned around it looked as if Terrance had somehow lost his footing and slipped off the edge of the building. It was like watching a scene from a movie in real time as his body fell through the air.

I covered my eyes.

No way could I ever watch my husband and the father of my unborn child die. I tried to recall a good memory, so that I wouldn't lose it out there in front of all those people, but it wasn't working. I felt lightheaded as the ground moved underneath my feet. My forehead began to sweat, and I suddenly grew cold. All the sound around me seemed to go on mute as I found myself slipping down to the ground. I saw people pointing and feet running towards me, and then everything was black.

Portia Chanel Jackson

This stupid bitch stopped me from saving the love of my life!

Watching Terrance plummet to the ground was heartbreaking. Tanya passed out and I couldn't get a grip on the thought of my baby daddy possibly being dead. I loved him. All I could think about was this nigga had to be out of his mind trying to kill his self before he even got a chance to hit this pussy again.

Yes, I said it. Don't judge me because I am addicted to my baby daddy's dick. That's why I give him a hard time whenever I see him. That redbone wife of his is no competition with me in the bedroom. I do shit to him that I know she wouldn't even dream of doing. That's why he keeps coming back to me.

I watched all of the paramedics and police run over to his body.

This just can't be over. I refuse to accept it.

I was just with Terrance a couple of weeks ago. I looked back to see firefighters and paramedics moving people out of the way so they could get a gurney through, and all I could do was sit on the sidewalk and hug myself. I could still feel Terrance's big hands as they roamed the curves on my body. I smelled the sweet mint lingering on his tongue as he kissed me. I tingled as I recalled the hot love making session we had.

*****

We were posted up at some swanky hotel across the street from his job site. Terrance grabbed my hips and thrust me down harder.

"Ahhhhhh….," I screamed.

"That's right, give it to daddy just the way I like it," he said.

I bucked like I was riding a horse hoping and praying I would get pregnant for the third time. I tried to leave marks on him while we made love, so that Tanya would see them and divorce him for cheating, but her dumbass would eventually find some way to forgive him.

When I dug my nails into his arm he froze.

"Get your nails out of my arm, or you will leave a mark," he said.

"I don't care," I replied nonchalant.

"I do," he said aggressively.

I sucked my teeth, moved my hand to the sheets, and held on tight. Terrance brought me to a sensual release over and over. That man surely knew what the hell he was doing. Once we were done, he paused for a second before preparing to move.

"No, please don't move," I pleaded.

I tried to tighten the grip my thighs had around his waist. Terrance pried my legs apart and moved to the edge of the bed. Rolling my eyes I sat up. He looked down at my body before he got up to discard the condom and went into the bathroom to wash up.

I hated when he did that because it always made me feel cheap, or even second, and Portia Chanel Jackson was never second. I didn't give a damn what anyone thought about it either.

"Terrance, I'm getting real tired of this," I said, the sound of desperation in my voice.

I heard the sound of the shower being turned on. I started pouting like a kid as I crossed my arms over my breasts.

When I looked on the nightstand I saw the light on his cell phone blinking. On the caller Id the words *my wife* flashed across the screen.

"Hey Terrance, your wife is calling you," I whispered.

Nothing would give me more joy than to pick up the phone and say hello to her since I hated her so much. I smiled as I thought about the look on her face when she heard the sound of my voice. Hitting the send button I listened first.

"Hello? Terrance is that you? Hello?"

Just as I was about to speak the phone was snatched out of my hand. Terrance gave me a nasty look. Still wet from the shower, he was wearing a towel around his waist. The bulge of his penis showed through the white, crisp towel. I licked my lips in anticipation for round two.

"Hey baby, sorry about that my phone doesn't get good reception in the building. Yes I'm still at work finishing up on a project."

I cleared my throat and he kicked me lightly with his foot.

"Ok thanks. I'll be on my way there. Alright, love you too."

He tossed his cell phone on the bed and began to rub his body down with coconut oil.

I tried to remove his towel and force him back into the bed with me. Terrance had skills when it came to sex. He used to do this thing with his tongue that had me curling my toes every single time.

"I wish you would have just married me so we wouldn't have to play this stupid game."

Once again I grabbed at the bulge underneath his towel.

"P, stop playing and move."

He grabbed my hand and pushed it to the side.

"How many times do you think I am going to keep doing this? We only have sex, and you never want to go anywhere. If it weren't for me having your kids, I honestly don't think you would even deal with me," I said.

He stayed silent while putting on his clothes.

The pain of his rejection hurt every time. I felt the tears in my eyes. I wanted to believe that Terrance had to feel something for me. He loved his kids and he loved my sex. That had to count for something right? Since he didn't want to acknowledge his feelings I had to hit him where I felt it would hurt him the most, his pockets. I dried my tears.

"I need $5000."

Terrance was bent over putting on his shoes. I watched his back stiffen as he rubbed his neck, a gesture he did when he was uncomfortable.

"Why? I just gave you money two days ago."

"Yea well TJ needs a new XBOX game, and Teyah is outgrowing her shoes, and I need some supplies for my shop."

"Don't you think $5000 is too much?" He put his left shoe on, paused and looked at me.

"Don't you think it costs to keep sleeping with me?" I said dropping the sheet so that my breasts would show. Terrance was an ass man, but I knew he liked my breasts too.

He stared at them before responding.

"Are you trying to tell me that you are turning tricks now?"

"Yup, I do tricks in the bed and you pay me for not telling your wife about where you really are on your lunch breaks." I scooted closer to him.

He sighed loudly.

"Portia, don't start that emotional bullshit right now."

"Why? Don't you think I deserve more than what you give me? Maybe Tanya needs to know what's really going on."

I grabbed my cell phone.

In the blink of an eye he put his hands around my neck and squeezed.

"If you even mention one word to my wife I will kill you do you understand?" Terrance screamed at me.

I was scared but surely I wasn't going to let him know that.

"Take your fucking hands off of me!"

Terrence released his grip and began to gather his things.

"You will never be happy will you? I fuck you good, take care of you, and my kids and you still aren't satisfied," he said more to himself than to me.

"I want more than just a quick fuck here and there," I sobbed.

Terrance was headed towards the door.

"You can't have more and you know that. We have been over this I don't know how many times."

"I knew you first," I pleaded.

"It doesn't matter. I love my wife."

I hated when he said that shit to me.

"Well then why are you still having sex with me?"

Terrance was silent. I felt a deep unsettling pain in my heart.

"Do you love me Terrance?"

He turned his back so I couldn't see the expression that had crossed his face.

"I love TJ and Teyah," he responded.

"I know that already. I asked do you love me?"

The seconds it took for him to give me an answer seemed like an eternity.

"No," he said flatly.

That word, those two letters stung. I felt like someone punched me in the stomach. I wanted him to love me. That was all. I had his kids and I thought that was enough to make him at least want to love me, or pretend he did even if it was a lie.

I wanted him to tell me that I wasn't just a baby mama that I was someone who mattered to him more than what my hips, and the walls of my vagina could do for him.

"I hate you!" I screamed out.

I picked up one of my heels and aimed for his head. He ducked just in time as it hit the wall. He ignored me and proceeded towards the door.

"You leave now and you will never see your kids again," I screamed.

Even though I was lying I wanted him to fight me back. I wanted him to yell, scream, or curse me out to let me know he cared. When I heard the slamming of the hotel door it confirmed what I already knew in my heart, he didn't give a fuck. In the end it never mattered that Terrance was married to Tanya. I didn't care. I had a piece of him which was his kids. For the next eighteen years he had to deal with me whether he wanted to or not. To me having that piece of a man was better than having no man at all. Now here I am sitting here with nothing but pieces of that man and a broken heart.

Amber Marie Sykowski

The ringing of my cell phone woke me up from a deep sleep.

"This better be good," I said groggily into my phone.

"Amber….?"

The voice on the other end was unfamiliar.

"Yes, who is this?" I asked.

"This is Portia."

"Portia, what the hell do you want?" I asked angered she had wakened me from my sleep.

"It's about Terrance," she said. The emotion in her voice was obvious. I sat upright in my bed and turned on the light sitting on my nightstand.

"What about Terrance? Portia what happened? Why are you crying?"

"He tried to kill himself and ….he fell from his office building," she began sobbing.

I got up pulling on my jeans and a t-shirt I found on the floor. I didn't want to ask her what I feared most, the father of my child being dead. The words caught in my throat.

"Is he...?" I couldn't bring myself to say it.

"No he isn't dead. He is in a coma. He is at Mercy hospital. It's not looking too good right now," I listened as she blew her nose.

Though I couldn't stand this woman I was happy she called to let me know.

"Alright I'm on my way," I said and hung up. I searched my closet for my tennis shoes.

I didn't know how I was supposed to feel. Part of me wanted to ask him what the hell he was thinking, and a very small part of me wanted to hold him. I am not sure why. I haven't been with Terrance in years.

Our son, Nathan, is thirteen years old, but they say you never forget your first. Terrance was my first love, the first to take my virginity, and the first black man I had ever dated. I endured abuse at the hands of my mother to be with Terrance, something many people never knew.

"Is everything okay?" My mother asked tapping on my door.

I moved back home with my son so I could save money to buy a house. My parents agreed to give me the down payment, but I had been so dependent on them I wanted to do something on my own for once. Since I was their only child they didn't mind.

It was the best thing for me to do at the time, but I started to regret that decision.

She let herself in my room.

"I thought you were taking a nap?" She said.

I gave her a half smile. She had her brown hair pulled tight into a bun in the back of her head which made her brown eyes look really tight and narrow giving her a very stern look.

"I was. I forgot I had some business I need to handle, so now I'm up. Everything is fine mom," I said casually.

There was no way I could tell her about Terrance. She hated him.

"No it isn't. You are going to see Nathan's father aren't you? I just heard what he did on the police scanner."

My mother was a sheriff and in her spare time even when not at work she listened to the police scanner.

"His ass is laid up in the hospital which serves him right," she said.

I heard her mumble the last part. I just shook my head. There was no point in getting her started because she never knew how to stop.

I couldn't understand why she was so mad since Terrance took care of Nathan financially. She always made it a point to try and one up him on every gift he gave him during birthdays and Christmas. Whenever Nathan went to his house for visits she would put up such a big fuss for no reason at all.

"Mom, I have to go can you grab Nate from school for me?" I asked.

"When will you stop pining away after that nigg-.....man?" My mother asked.

I swung my head around almost daring her to say the word. I grabbed my keys from the table and walked out the room without answering her.

I hopped in my car and drove straight to the hospital still upset at my mother's choice of words. My son was half black and I was offended by the way she was carrying on about his black father.

I felt a tear on my cheek as I drove to the hospital. Terrance could not be dead. I wasn't going to allow myself to think negatively.

Pulling into the hospital parking lot, I pulled up to the valet, handed them the keys, and walked slowly through the doors praying everything would be alright. When I got to the nurse's station I found myself stuttering and unable to form the words I needed to say.

Could I still be in love after all these years?

After forcing myself to speak, the nurse directed me to Terrance's room, room 222.

I tried to ignore the pounding of my heart as I walked down the fluorescent lit hallway. The smell of bleach and the cold chill in the air made me wrap my arms around myself. Walking up, I heard the sound of Portia and Tanya's voice inside. The two of them together was a bomb waiting to detonate. I made the smart decision to wait in the adjacent waiting room to gather my thoughts, and to let go of any feelings I was holding on to after all these years. There was no way I could walk in like this and try to act normal. The minute Tanya looked in my face she would know everything. She would know that I still loved her husband very much, and that I wouldn't stop at anything to let him know that before he left this earth.

Terrance

"Doctor I think you may want to come in here. He seems to be pulling through."

The sound of the woman's voice was distant in my head but I heard it. I tried to move my hand but couldn't. Only my fingers moved. I heard a beeping sound coming from some machine. I tried to open my eyes but something was holding them together. I was sure I was dead because I started to remember certain things about my life like the day the doctor told me I was dying.

*****

I had to visit my doctor for a follow up appointment for my test results. When I walked in the waiting room, the front desk receptionist flashed me a smile and said,

"Terrance Davenport, the doctor will see you now."

"That was fast don't I have to sign in?" I asked.

"No don't bother I already know who you are. Besides, we are slow today so go on back."

She smiled again and I thought I saw her pink tongue slide across her dry, lipstick covered lips. I was accustomed to women going above and beyond for me, but she reminded me of my grandmother, so the thought of what she wanted to offer me was sickening.

When I entered the room the doctor was already inside flipping on the light to the X-ray viewing machine.

"Terrance, good to see you come on in and have a seat on the table."

I sat down on the white, paper covered exam table. My doctor was an older Caucasian man with gray hair. He was the best pulmonary doctor in all of Chicago. He grabbed the stool and pulled it close to me looking me in the eye.

"How have you been feeling?" He asked.

"Besides the pain in my chest I am okay," I responded.

He paused and wrote down some notes in my file.

"The cancer is a lot worse than we expected. I know we said with the last surgery we had got most of the cancer cells out, but looking at your film you have some clots forming underneath your right lung. That would be the cause of your chest pains. The cancer has now progressed to stage IV. We cannot stop the progression of it since it will begin to attack your vital organs. If you see this area right here," the Dr. pointed to the middle of the x-ray. "This is your heart. In the next few months the cancer will have spread causing your heart to overwork and it could eventually stop beating."

I stared at him. All the words I wanted to say were caught in my throat.

"Am I going to die?" I asked.

"We can start you on some chemotherapy and pain medication to keep you comfortable. At the rate of progression, you have maybe six to eight months, maybe even a year or more. It is hard to give you an exact day. Every case is different. You can possibly beat it and live longer than that. It's up to your body and how long it can continue to fight the cancer."

I couldn't believe it!

"Doc, I'm really going to die?" I was in utter shock.

He gave me a sorrowful look.

"I can't really say Terrance. I'm sorry. I can only give you my medical advice and opinion. I will say you might want to make some preparations with your wife just for you know…insurance."

I stared at my feet. He delivered me a death sentence and I couldn't swallow it.

"I know this isn't easy at all. Would you like the nurse to call your wife?"

I shook my head.

"I'm so sorry Terrance. Here is the number for the pain management and radiation treatment clinic. Please make an appointment with them as soon as possible. I'll send the nurse in with some information for you."

The doctor left the room leaving me alone to my thoughts.

My feet felt cemented to the floor and my body felt like a ton of bricks.

I felt a drop of water on my hand. I didn't even realize there were tears slipping down my cheeks. I heard a light tap at the door before a nurse entered the room.

"Mr. Davenport, I came to give you a number to a support group that can help you deal with this."

I looked at the brown-skinned nurse with the pixie hair cut. She placed the card in my hand. I took one look at it and began to laugh. She looked up at me and frowned.

"What makes you think I want to talk about this shit?"

I stood up and found my six foot, four inch frame towering right over the petite nurse. She backed up slowly.

"I am leaving four kids and a woman who I have done nothing but disappoint. How do you think I feel going home to let her know I'm dying?"

My anger began to replace my sadness. Before I realized it I pushed over the cart containing supplies, sending it crashing to the floor. I watched the nurse jump out the way and press the help button on the wall.

"Calm down Mr. Davenport, please!" She begged.

"For what, you have no idea how I feel right now!"

The nurse frowned before dropping her head.

A male nurse peeked inside the room.

"Is everything okay in here Rene?" He asked.

She put her hand up and nodded her head. I looked at the male nurse.

"Oh excuse me; am I taking up too much time? Fuck me I'm just dying! I will be gone in no time, and you will have one less patient to deal with!"

I kicked the stool on wheels and sent it flying into the wall.

"Mr. Davenport, enough with the tantrum! I understand the difficulty you are experiencing right now, I do! The best advice I can give you is to go home to your family and enjoy all the moments you can. Take my advice if you have any money, put it aside for your children. Please take the time to handle it, and once you get a grasp of it start preparing your family for it."

The nurse walked out the door.

I dropped down to my knees as more tears fell from my face. I wasn't supposed to be dying. I was still young.

"Mr. Davenport can you hear the sound of my voice?" I wasn't sure if I was still dreaming or if this was reality.

I heard the male voice echoing in the background.

Was this heaven?

No, definitely not. Anyone who committed suicide I was sure went straight to hell. It was a sin in the bible.

"Terrance? Terrance baby can you hear me?"

The melodic voice was familiar and sweet. I heard another voice and felt hands on my skin.

"His vitals are stable and he seems to be regaining consciousness. Let's observe him over the next forty-eight hours and see how he comes out of the coma."

A coma? At least I wasn't dead yet.

I wanted to shake my head, but I couldn't will it to move. I guess God wasn't done with me yet. I remember being on the ledge of my office building. I was sure I was ready to die, but yet I am still here, so I must be one lucky muthafucka.

Once the tape was removed, I was able to open my eyes and saw a blurry face come into view. I blinked a few times to bring the image into focus. Her smile lit up the entire room.

"Hey you," she said.

Tears instantly sprang to my eyes. My wife's face was a sight for sore eyes. Once again I tried to move my hand. This time she noticed the movement of my fingers and grabbed my hand into hers. She touched my palm to her face and I felt the soft skin on her cheek.

"You tried to leave me. You tried to leave us," she whispered.

I watched as the tears came to her eyes as she moved my hand down to her stomach. I felt bad. I tried to open my mouth to say I was sorry, but something was caught in my throat. The doctor leaned over to examine me.

"Terrance, we'll get that breathing tube out in a few so you can talk," he said.

I nodded my head thankful my brain had finally caught up.

"That was quite a fall you took there. If it weren't for you falling on top of that fireman you wouldn't be here."

My eyes widened at the thought of me killing someone else.

The doctor seemed to read my mind.

"Don't worry the fireman is going to be fine. He had a slight concussion and some bruises, but he broke some of your fall. You hit your head pretty bad which is how you slipped into the coma."

I noticed movement towards the door and saw my baby mama, Portia, was now standing in the room. She was dressed like she was about to be in someone's music video. I could always count on her to let me know my dick wasn't dead. I felt the blood rush to my pelvis as her titties bounced in her shirt. This was not going to be good. I fought back the lust gathering in my loins fearful my wife would see. I watched Tanya approach cautiously.

"What the hell are you doing here?" I heard Tanya try to whisper.

"What do you think I'm doing here? I brought my kids to see their father," Portia replied through gritted teeth.

At the mention of my kids, I looked over to see my son Terrance Jr. was hiding behind his mother, and my daughter Teyah was burying her face in her shoulder.

"I don't think they should see him like this," Tanya said.

I couldn't agree with her more. I didn't want my kids to have to visit me like this.

"Who are you to tell me what my kids need to see? When you actually have your baby you can relate to what a mother feels until then, shut the fuck up and move out of my way," Portia said.

I watched her try to step past Tanya, but Tanya wasn't having it. She blocked her path.

I closed my eyes wishing I could morph away from the both of them. There had to be some way to make them get along.

"What type of mother are you to bring your kids to a hospital and then act a fool?"

I reached out to grab Tanya's hand to calm her down, but the pain I felt in my head and chest was too great.

"Girl, get out of my face so I can see my baby daddy," Portia said stepping around her.

I watched as she came to the side of my bed. My eyes stayed on Tanya until I felt the soft press of Portia's lips to my cheek.

"I thought you were dead baby," she whispered. My eyes widened in horror. I prayed that Tanya didn't hear or see what had just happened. The room grew deathly quiet. I saw Tanya's hand move, but it didn't register that she slapped Portia until I heard her say,

"Bitch, you have a lot of nerve to come up here in this hospital and put your nasty lips on my husband's cheek right in front of my face!"

Helplessly, I watched Portia set my daughter down and lunge herself into Tanya, sending her flying into the wall. I heard my daughter screaming as the two of them tousled back and forth in my hospital room.

Several nurses and security came in the room to break them apart.

"You both have to leave this hospital right now!" One of the nurses shouted.

"She started it," I heard Portia say.

"And I'm finishing it both of you get your stuff and get out before I have to call the police," the security grabbed Portia by her arm.

"Get off of me you flashlight cop I have to get my baby," Portia yelled.

Teyah was crying. I looked over at TJ and he had his head hanging down with his lip poked out. All I could do was shake my head back and forth. This was ridiculous. I knew Portia was a hood chic when I started messing with her, but when she came around my wife she brought things out of Tanya I didn't even know she was capable of. It was as if Tanya and Portia were two pit bulls always trying to lock their jaws around each other's necks.

"Fucking rent-a-cop ass, don't touch me no more," Portia said to the security officer waiting by the door.

I saw my son's mother, Amber appear in the doorway. Tanya and Portia rolled their eyes at the same time. I shut my eyes and prayed this was just a bad nightmare and that when I opened my eyes everything would be back to normal. That was not the case.

Portia gave Amber the side eye as she snatched up my kids.

"What took yo' ass so long to get here? I called you over an hour ago!"

Amber turned up her face. She was not one for any type of drama, so Portia's in- your- face attitude was never received well.

"Excuse me I didn't know I was being timed. If you have to know, I was sleep when you called," Amber responded.

"Ha, like you have a job! You live with your damn momma and daddy, so what you so tired from, spending all their money?" Portia asked,

"Is there ever one time that you aren't full of drama? Look at you, we are all here for the same reason, but yet you always have to be over the top," Amber replied while trying to move past Portia.

I felt caught in the middle of a reality show that I didn't sign up for.

"Portia get out of her face before I help her mop the floor with your ass," Tanya answered.

"Don't say another word to me because you are one step from getting your pregnant ass beat again."

"I wish you would," Tanya said.

"Alright ladies your time is up," the security officer said while ushering them out of my room.

Portia turned on her heels and headed into the hallway.

Tanya mouthed the words "I'm sorry," kissed me on my forehead and exited the room.

"You too miss lady," the security officer said to Amber.

"What? I just got here," she said with too much emotion in her voice.

I had to intervene on her behalf.

"Can she stay for a while longer? She wasn't fighting?"

"Wait Tanya and Portia were fighting? In your hospital room? How ghetto!"

I frowned at Amber calling my wife ghetto. I could tell she sensed my dissatisfaction with her choice of words.

"I'm sorry T, you know I'm referring to Portia."

The security guard nodded her head and left the room. I could hear protest from Portia in the hallway once she found out Amber was allowed to stay.

It's all good. Thanks for coming. How is Nate doing?" I asked.

"He is good. He is at school. I …I didn't tell him what happened. I wanted to come see for myself," she replied.

I instantly felt regret for my actions.

"I'm sorry Amber," I said softly.

"No need to apologize. Just glad you are alive," She responded.

There was visible emotion present in her voice that I never heard before. I was never in an exclusive relationship with Amber, but I knew she still had feelings for me since she had my son.

There was an awkward silence between us.

"Are you still friends with Rebecca Smith?" I asked.

"Yes of course you know she is my best friend."

"I need her number. I have something I need to discuss with her."

"Okay."

I continued holding her hand. A flood of emotions coursed through my body and I wasn't sure what they meant. Amber and I hadn't been together in years. I knew I was the first to take her virginity and that alone gave us a special connection. You never forget your first!

The doctor knocked on the door interrupting my thoughts and shyly I let her hand go.

"I'm sorry I didn't realize you had a visitor," the doctor said. "I wanted to check your vitals again and talk about your CT scan." The doctor looked from me back to Amber.

"She can stay," I said softly and she smiled the warmest smile at me and took a seat near my bed.

Tanya

To say I was furious would be putting my feelings lightly. I was in a rage. How dare that ghetto ass broad show up and show out in my husband's hospital room? I don't give a damn if they had twenty children together she had no right to disrespect me to my face like that. She walked over and kissed him like she had been doing it on a regular basis. Then had the nerve to call him baby in my face like I didn't hear her whisper that shit! I had no doubt now that he was still fucking her.

I floored my BMW down the street until I reached the highway ramp that said I-94. I merged with traffic and drove until I found myself headed towards Milwaukee, Wisconsin. I exited right and jumped off the interstate, turning my car back in the opposite direction. I felt the tears stinging my eyes as they forced their way out. I had to pull over on the side of the road to gain my composure. I hit the steering wheel.

"Am I supposed to divorce him now and just let her take my husband from me?"

I was talking to myself again.

Hate is a strong word to use, but I am starting to hate this girl. I think I hate her more for having not one, but two of my husband's kids, than I hate her for being the ghetto tramp she was raised to be. Before I realized how fast I was driving, I ended up back at home in less than ten minutes, which was a record compared to the normal twenty minutes it took. I parked my car in the underground garage got out, locked it, and stomped my way over to the elevator.

Using my special key to activate the elevator I stood there with my arms folded across my stomach. I took the elevator up to the ninth floor of our loft apartment and stomped down the hallway all the way to my door.

"Damn it all to hell!"

I said out loud as I stubbed my toe on a chair while walking in my house. Sitting down on the end of the couch I tried to rub my foot. Bending over with a pregnant belly was difficult and required some effort. I was damn near out of breath once I stood back up.

I walked through the empty living room, glancing at my wedding picture sitting on the mantle over the fireplace. In the picture, I had a flower in my hair while wearing a beautiful pink sundress. Terrance had on a white linen pant suit and we were flanked by both of our parents on both sides. All of the anger I felt previously, melted away as I stared at the picture.

When I first met Terrance I thought I struck gold. We both were born and raised in Chicago, Illinois and went to Oak Park River Forest high school. Coincidentally, we also ended up attending the same college, Clark University in Atlanta, Georgia. Terrance was popular in school, and was very much a ladies' man. Every female on campus wanted to be with Terrance McCall Davenport. He was six four; with a chocolate complexion, freckles, a killer smile, and a slight Jamaican accent. He also had the body of an athlete. I was intimidated at first by his popularity since I wasn't an outgoing person at all. I kept to myself and spoke only to people I knew.

I was pretty much a nerd who wore braces. I would see him in the campus cafeteria talking to his friends and I couldn't do anything but watch him. He played basketball and always had a flock of people around who wanted to be in his presence. People said he was headed to the NBA.

With potential NBA fame, groupies came by the dozens.

He had a very addictive personality. Once he started talking to you, you wanted him to keep on talking forever. The words he spoke dripped off his lips like honey maple syrup on a warm pancake.

Terrance was never alone for a few minutes without some chic sliding him her number, or hanging on to his every word as he talked. I watched from a distance as he almost lived out his dream of going pro until he blew out his knee his junior year.

I was there at the clinic working, when the doctor came in and examined him, letting him know he had torn his ACL in his knee and would have to undergo surgery. This would put him out of the chances of going pro until he recovered. Later on, once they went in, they found he had irreparable nerve damage. His career in sports was over before it truly began. He had to go through months of intensive physical therapy and started to withdraw from the public eye. For months the media talked about losing the best player they had seen in a long time. A few months had passed before he started coming out of his depression. I tried to avoid running in to him, but he seemed to have my schedule down to a science. Every time he saw me he asked me out and I turned him down each and every time. I told him I refused to date anyone in college who was a former athlete, because I had heard all of the stories. There was no way I could compete with what he was accustomed to getting from all the groupies that used to come around. Eventually, a friendship formed and we became the best of friends.

He would have me laughing about all the girls who would show up in his room naked or wearing next to nothing just so he could sleep with them. Even though he was no longer Terrance the athlete, he was still Terrance Davenport, and his last name had money behind it.

Everyone knew his parents had money and his father was a self-made millionaire, so one could assume the qualities or the money would pass on to his son.

Women were desperate to be with him, slipping me notes with their numbers on it, or telling me to take a picture of them and post it in his dorm room for them.

The more our friendship grew the fear of falling in love with him scared me.

Each time I asked him what his plans were now that he was no longer playing basketball; he would just look at me, smile and say,

"I'm going to marry you and have a bunch of kids."

I would nervously laugh it off until finally one day he stop saying it, so I replied back out of the blue,

"You have to date me first."

I remembered how he paused and gazed deep, and lovingly into my eyes which scared the crap out of me.

After we had been dating exclusively for a year, Terrance called my dad and asked for my hand in marriage. He proposed on Valentine's Day right in the middle of the campus school yard in front of everyone. He had the school band play Jodeci's song, Forever My Lady, while he got down on one knee. Terrance promised to take care of me like my father took care of my sister and me. Since Terrance was a year ahead of me, he was set to graduate from college first before I was.

He received word right before his college graduation ceremony that he had secured the civil engineer, trainee position at a big company back home in Chicago. This meant a lot to him since it would set up his future to provide for our life together.

Terrance spoiled me every chance he got. He sent me flowers, bought my lunch, took me shopping and he even bought my first car. He made sure I finished my nursing program at school and was there cheering me on when I walked across the stage. I was in heaven. I felt love in a way that I had never experienced in my life.

When my mother suddenly passed away from a massive heart attack, it was Terrance that paid for my plane ticket back home to Chicago. He was there to hold my hand and assisted my family every step of the way with anything that we needed.

That was the most important thing to me and it was then that I knew he was the one I should marry. I was more than overjoyed to become Mrs. Terrance Davenport and I wore that title proudly.

I put the picture back down, wiped the tears from my face and placed my hands on my belly.

"Don't worry baby we are going to be alright," I said out loud.

I was determined not to let Portia or anyone else take from me what I worked so hard to maintain.

Terrance

One week later

After being put on suicide watch for a week I was finally released from the hospital when the doctors were convinced I was no longer a threat to myself. I had to put my plan into gear. Being in that hospital room reminded me of the *man* I was supposed to be. I wasn't raised to be weak.

In my childhood years I was the respectful young man my parents taught me to be. Born and raised in Kingston, Jamaica my parents came to the states when I was ten years old. They moved my two siblings and me to Chicago, Illinois. We didn't struggle much because my parents knew how to get money. It didn't matter if they had to hold down two and three jobs, they made sure we were cared for.

My father was a genius when it came to working on cars and owned many car shops throughout the Tri-state area of Wisconsin, Illinois, and Indiana. He had no college degree, but he was good with his hands. He became a self-made millionaire when he developed a machine that would assist every mechanic in the world with diagnostic repairs on any foreign or domestic automobile.

My mother too, was a woman of many talents. She could braid hair, run a nursing home, attend PTA meetings, cook meals for the homeless, feed us, go to church, and still have time to keep us all in line.

My parents were big on family and keeping them together. If you had a problem, we had a family meeting about it, and resolved it together. I was always taught to be there for my younger brother and sister at all times no matter what.

When I was a junior in high school, my parents started talking real heavy about going to college. I knew it was a big thing to them since I would be the first Davenport boy to have more than an elementary school education. I kept my grades above average, and filled out every scholarship application, and grant there was available.

When it came to finding something I was good at, it was sports and sex. I know that may sound a bit exaggerated, but it's true. I was a pro at playing basketball, and made it my business to hit the courts all throughout high school. Being good at sex came later on. After the girl who took my virginity as a teenager told me I wasn't shit, I made it my business to learn how to please a woman in every way imaginable. I read books on sex and asked my dad every question under the sun. Dad would always say in his heavy Jamaican accent, *"boy always have control over da dick, put da woman first when it comes to pleasure and you will never go wrong."*

Every girl wanted to be with me once they learned I was an athlete, so the attention came by the dozens. I reveled in it sometimes dating two or three different girls at once. Some were cool not being number one, but the mother's of my children were not.

Amber was the first white girl I ever dated. I caught the side eye every now and then from the other black girls at school. Her mother hated my guts, but I believed that was only because I was black.

I used to make up this fantasy notion in my head that Amber's mother secretly wanted me for herself that's why she never wanted us together. The myth about black men having a big dick was true in my case and I knew she was curious.

When Amber came up pregnant with my son, I made the decision to stop being a player and take care of my responsibility. My determination to get a scholarship paid off and I landed a full ride to Clark University, in Atlanta, Georgia.

I tried to be around while she was pregnant, but with me being in school in Atlanta, and with her back home in Chicago it was hard. I never wanted my son to grow up without a father, and it hurt me to my core when her family did everything in their power to keep my son away from me. It wasn't until Nathan was old enough to talk and ask for me that they cut me some slack.

Instead of asking Tanya to pick me up from the hospital today, I asked my brother to come and get me. I had to take care of a few things without Tanya's emotional pregnant ass asking me twenty questions, or doting on me.

I knew what I did was hard on her, but she would never understand what led me to do it.

My first stop was to Attorney Rebecca Smith's office to discuss my plan. Her office was located in the west loop of Chicago on Washington Street near Harpo Studios, which was Oprah Winfrey's office.

Upon running down my plan to her, Rebecca was silent.

"Do you think this will work?" I asked her.

I sat upright in the black, high backed, chair across from her trying not to stare at her perky, double D breasts.

I watched as she crossed her arms over her chest as if she knew I was watching. Her neatly pressed white shirt was open just enough to show the crack of her cleavage. She crossed her feet at the ankles as she leaned back in her chair. Rebecca was strikingly attractive with her curvy hips, shoulder length blonde hair, and her ocean blue colored eyes. Rebecca and I messed around one time when we were teenagers right before I met Amber. When I found out they were best friends I had to leave one of them alone. Sadly, it was the one with the biggest breasts.

After pausing for an eternity she finally answered my question.

"In my professional opinion yes it could. If you could somehow get them all to sign their names agreeing to this "*Arrangement*" as you call it, it will be a legal binding contract."

I paused, mulling this thought over in my mind. I wanted this to be as smooth and painless as possible.

I watched as she folded her hands in her lap and stared out the floor to ceiling window.

"Penny for your thoughts", I said.

Rebecca turned her chair towards me and removed the glasses from her eyes before she spoke.

"Terrance, I have known you since high school. I know that you have always had a way with women, so getting what you want has never been a problem. I also know that what you are asking of these women is almost ridiculous if not absurd."

"How is that? I am not asking for blood or money. I am asking them to do one simple thing that will be for the benefit of my children. They won't have to worry about a thing but raising my kids."

Rebecca smirked.

"That is not how they will see it. You are asking three women with whom you currently have, and have had a sexual relationship with at one time, and produced children with, to come together and live under one roof. I don't honestly see how you think that this can possibly work. They are going to think you have lost your mind. I know I do!"

I pushed my chair away from the table and stood up. I shook my head as I smiled at her.

"I thought you would understand why I have to do this. This is to protect the kids in my ....absence," I said softly.

Rebecca stood up and walked over to me, casually sitting on the edge of her desk. She was wearing a black pencil skirt that accentuated her hips. It was hard to concentrate with her sitting so close to me.

"You can turn off the charm now. I am not interested. This sounds more like control if you ask me." She leaned in closer giving me a full view of the top of her cleavage. This felt like a game of seduction that we both were playing. I licked my lips while she spoke. "Admit it; you want the upper hand in their lives even in the event of your death."

I could smell the freshness of her breath as she spoke. I tried to stay focused, speaking silently to my other head to stay down.

"No, I don't. It's for my children," I reminded her.

The scent of her perfume filled my nostrils. I took a deep breath, drinking in her intoxicating fragrance.

She let out a hearty laugh.

"Ok, Terrance if you say so, it's for the children! Have you even once stopped to consider how this will affect everyone including the children?" She asked.

I looked deep into her blue eyes, the lust continually building up in my loins. I pictured her draped over a chair while I hit it from the back, smacking her ass, as her nails scratched her mahogany colored desk.

Clearing my throat and that image from my head I said,

"Of course and that's why I think it's the perfect arrangement," I said confidently.

"Sounds like you have it all figured out."

"I do. Now if you agree to represent me and make sure my plans are followed through accordingly, I will compensate you *very* well." I put an emphasis on the last part.

She bit her bottom lip and gave me a sexy look. I wanted badly to fuck her again. From the body language she was throwing me, I could tell she wanted it too.

She smiled and moved closer until we were inches apart.

"Yes, you will compensate very well at my asking price! You are lucky I know you, otherwise I'd tell you to take your arrangement and go to hell. Since I believe your wife and your kids' mothers are going to give you an earful, I'll just leave all the choice words to them." She turned to walk on the other side of her desk giving me a full view of her ass.

I grabbed her hand and pulled her close to me. I let her feel how hard she had my dick from this game she was playing. I felt her body stiffen as I lifted her palm to my lips and kissed it softly. I heard her take in a breath as she snatched it away. Her body language was screaming *fuck me now, right here*.

There was a silence as she stared at me with lust dripping from the unspoken words lingering in the air. I watched as she tried to keep her composure.

"Goodbye Terrance and good luck. I'll be in touch with the paperwork," she finally said.

I winked as I left her office. I glanced back over my shoulder and noticed her fanning herself. I should have taken advantage of the opportunity to fuck her on her desk. I don't have long to live so might as well live out my fantasies.

When I got outside my brother, Ty was waiting for me in my truck. He took one look at my face and said,

"Rebecca still fine as ever isn't she?"

I nodded my head and gave him some pound with my fist.

Man her body still on point even after all these years. I wish some women would realize that if you take care of your body, a man will always want you no matter how much time has passed." Pausing, I thought about Rebecca again. "Take me home man, before I go back up there and knock a hole in that pussy."

My brother laughed.

"Bro, you are a wild boy."

He pulled out of the parking lot and headed to my house.

Pulling up to the loft apartment I shared with Tanya in the heart of downtown Chicago, my brother hit the button for the underground garage and parked my F-150 in my designated parking spot. I looked around the garage as I got out of my truck and closed my door. The smell of gas was evident in the air. I noticed my neighbor was parked in my wife's parking spot again, but I didn't care. Normally I would march right up to his door and make him move, but today that wasn't even important.

"If you need me to stay while you talk to Tanya I can. I know after you tell her about this *arrangement* you came up with, pots and pans might get to flying," Ty said.

I looked my little brother in the eyes. He was the spitting image of my father with his high cheekbones and masculine features. He had curly hair and freckles on his nose like my mother.

"Naw man that's alright, thank you for bringing me home, tell mom I will call her and not to worry."

"You had us scared for a moment. We thought we were going to lose you," I could hear him choking back his emotions.

"Yeah I know."

The regret I felt at the hospital returned. My actions had affected the people I loved in more ways than one.

There was a silence between us.

My brother gave me a hug.

"I love you man," he said.

"I love you too; now get out of here before someone sees us hugging."

He laughed and got into his car.

I put my key into the slot to activate the elevator. When the doors opened, out stepped my old neighbor from two doors down, Ms. Lee.

"Hey there Terry I just seen that wife of yours. Pregnancy sure does her well."

She always called me Terry and never Terrance for some reason.

She looked at me like a mother would look at her child. I was waiting on her to scold me about the ledge incident. Thankfully she didn't.

"What's wrong boy?"

"Oh nothing, how are you doing Ms. Lee?" I asked.

"I'm old that's how I am. Everything hurts and I can't see like I used to without these glasses," she said pointing to the thick bifocals on her face.

Ms. Lee reminded me of my grandmother. She had to be in her seventies, but she got around like a woman of forty years.

She touched my hand and when I looked down at her light brown colored hands I noticed her fingers were old and wrinkled.

"Life is short boy, hold on to what you can and leave the other shit alone."

She looked over the rim of her glasses at me and raised her eyebrows. I had to laugh. Hearing her curse was quite amusing.

"Ms. Lee you take care and tell your son I said hello."

I moved around her and got on the elevator praying the doors would close before she could say anything else. Hitting the button for the ninth floor I took a deep breath and tried to prepare myself for what I was going to say to Tanya about this *"Arrangement"*.

When I got to the door of my apartment I could smell the scent of cheese tortellini and garlic bread in the air. Ever since Tanya found out she was pregnant she stayed in the kitchen whipping up every dish she could think of.

I put the key in the door turning the knob ever so slightly trying not to alert her of my presence.

"Hey babe I'm in the kitchen," she called out.

So much for trying to buy myself time to pull it all together.

"Be right there sweetie. I'm going to use the bathroom."

I slipped into the half bath we had down the hall just off the living room. I turned on the faucet to drown out the call I was getting ready to make.

"Hey, Portia its Terrance can you come by? No, not for that I have something important to talk to you about. ......I don't need to hear all that just bring your ass by my house in the next hour. Why can't you ever listen? Just come by, damn!"

I ended the call and dialed another number.

"Hey, Amber I need to talk to you about a matter of importance and I need you at my house in the next hour. .....Yes this is very important. Okay, see you soon."

I shoved my cell phone in my pocket, flushed the toilet, and turned off the water. I looked at the cream colored hand towels with our initials engraved on them in orange, which were on the towel rack, as I dried my hands. For the first time I noticed the way Tanya had the towels neatly folded. I decided to fold them back just the way she had them when normally I wouldn't give a damn about something so simple.

I approached the kitchen slowly. I could see Tanya's back was turned as she moved back and forth across the stove turning eyes down and stirring sauces. She was wearing one of my t-shirts and a pair of jogging pants. I watched as the flesh on the back of her arms jiggled a little as she moved. Her shoulder length hair was pulled up in a high ponytail on the top of her head. She must have felt me staring at her because shc turned around and smiled.

"Hey baby! Glad to have you back home. I missed you."

She walked over to me and opened her arms closing me in a tight embrace. I hugged her and gave her a very long and passionate kiss while palming the back of her round ass.

"Wow, baby you need to stay in the hospital more, so I can always get a greeting like that when you come home."

I saw the expression of regret as soon as the words left her mouth.

Ignoring her comment, I unbuttoned her shirt to expose her skin. I planted kisses on her breasts and then moved down to her bulging stomach. I knelt down to the floor so that my face was near her belly button.

"Hey little man it's your daddy talking. I'm sorry I almost left you alone before you even got a chance to meet me. I promise you daddy won't do that again."

I choked back the tears I felt burning my eyelids. I continued to kiss along the sides of her stomach until my face was near the triangle of passion I loved so much. I tugged her jogging pants from around her waist and slid them down to her knees. I put my nose right between her thighs and inhaled deeply. Tanya moaned. I moved her panties down to where her jogging pants were and proceeded to lick the hairless fold of skin covering her vagina. She had gotten one of those Brazilian wax jobs that made her skin smooth and stubble free.

Tanya stroked my head while I licked the center of her mound.

"Baby, are you sure you don't want to rest after being in the h...hospital...I made your favorite dish," she said tenderly in between moans.

I shook my head and tried to focus. The lust I had from earlier needed to be released. I looked up to see the pleasure on her face. She was holding on to my head, her eyes rolling, and her toes curling into the tiled kitchen floor. My hands found their way back up to her breasts, as I twisted each nipple just the way she liked it. Her legs trembled as I continued to gently suck and lick her center causing her to create a puddle of her love juice on my shirt. She pulled my face in closer and I knew she was on the verge of an orgasm. Her moaning increased and grew louder which was driving me crazy. I pushed her up and on top of the counter placing both of her thighs on my shoulder. I thought I felt my son kick me in the head at one point. I moved back, inserted two fingers and rubbed the little button at the top of her pelvic bone with my middle finger.

My father always said once you find a woman's G-spot you have struck gold.

"Oh my gawddd, Terrance you know that's my spot!"

I loved the way she moaned my name. I stopped not wanting her to reach her peak just yet. Tanya's eyes flipped open and she started pouting in disappointment. I wasn't sure if I could sustain an erection long enough after all the medicine they pumped into me at the hospital.

When I stood up from being on my knees and saw my man sticking out hard, stiff and long, I smiled, and almost clapped, while gently pulling Tanya close turning her around so her back was to me. She wiggled her ass towards me wanting me to enter her from behind. It was the only way we could have sex comfortably since she was pregnant. I watched as she reached back and pulled down my pants and boxers in one fluid motion. I slid all ten, thick, inches inside of her and pumped in and out, grabbing her hair, turning her face so she could look at me. It was something about looking into a woman's eyes while you gave her the pleasure she needed. This time was different. I fought back the tears looking into her big, beautiful, brown eyes, filled with pleasure. I didn't want this moment to end.

This may be my last time I get to make love to my wife.

Sounds of skin slapping and moaning could be heard as we made love in the kitchen. Tanya arched her back and began to throw it back faster and harder at me until I had to hold on to her hips. She was trying to prove a point. This was her dick! I felt her insides began to tighten against me, and I knew she was getting ready to have an orgasm. She moaned while she tried to hold on to the counter. I held on to her hips for dear life. I slammed into her wet abyss, over and over like my life depended on it, until I felt the heat rising up from my toes. I locked in and thrust deeper, harder, and faster so that she could explode with me. Sweat beaded on my forehead as I clenched my teeth trying to hold back until I couldn't hold back any longer. Her vaginal walls tightened around my dick and I finally exploded into a much needed release.

I collapsed on her back holding her tightly to my chest. My hands moved down over her belly as I felt the small movement of my son. There was silence between us as I held her tighter, my tears falling on her back.

After about five minutes I stood up and turned her around to look at her.

"You are so beautiful," I kissed her forehead.

She smiled at me, sweat running down her face, as she tried to straighten her messed up ponytail. I forced myself to smile when I really wanted to cry.

"Tanya, I need to talk to you about something!"

A look of worry came across her face as I continued,

"I know a lot has happened and I haven't had a chance to really talk to you about it. I know I should have done that instead of climbing onto the ledge of that building." I choked back the tears that kept trying to fall from my eyes. "The cancer is progressing as you know and the doctor told me I am moving to stage four. I am going to eventually die."

I watched her closely for a reaction.

"No Terrance, I don't want to hear this. Not now." She threw her hands up in protest and turned her face away from me to hide her emotions.

I grabbed her face in my hands kissing her lips softly. I kissed the tears away that began to fall from her face. I felt her body relax.

"Please. It has to be now. We don't have time to put this off."
I regretted what I was going to say next. I took a deep breath before
continuing, "I invited Portia and Amber over, because I need all of
you present for what I have to say."

I watched a look of disgust spread across my wife's face at
the mention of their names.

"Terrance, why do we have to do this with them? Why? They
aren't married to you I am! You just got home from the hospital and
now this? This is a lot to deal with." She started rummaging around
in the kitchen drawer while mumbling under her breath, "Where is
my gun? I know I'm going to need it for Portia's mouth."

I gave her a look at the mention of a gun.

"I'm sorry babe. This was a last minute decision...."

The doorbell interrupted me.

"That must be them now," I said and left the kitchen to
answer the door.

I washed my hands in the bathroom and tried to wipe the
sweat from my body with a towel, not wanting it to be so obvious
that I had just had sex. I grabbed the cheap Axe Chocolate body
spray under the cabinet and sprayed a little on my chest and shirt to
mask any hint of love making.

I pressed the buzzer to activate the elevator and waited in the
hallway. I knew Tanya was pissed that I didn't warn her ahead of
time, but I didn't have much time. I needed to get everything situated
now before it was too late.

Portia was the first one to arrive. I watched as she walked down the hall swaying her hips side to side, as if she were walking down a fashion runway. Her long hair weave was pulled up in a high ponytail on top of her head. She had on a pair of tight ass skinny jeans, a top that made her breasts sit up, five inch stilettos, a big red purse, and a pair of Dolce & Gabbana sunglasses. My dick almost got hard again watching the way her titties bounced up and down in her shirt. If my wife wasn't home I'd put her ass against the wall and fuck the shit out of her. I had to focus.

I could hear her cracking her gum loudly as she got closer.

"What is so important that you made me leave my shop Terrance, and why do you look like you just came back from the gym? Didn't you just get out of the hospital?"

She sniffed the air and looked over the top of her glasses.

"Did you have to spray on the entire bottle of Axe, damn?"

She covered her nose with her hand.

"Hello to you too Portia just go right on in and have a seat."

I pointed to the door.

She looked at me and shook her head.

"Hell no, now you know that ain't happening. I will stand right here and enter behind you. I go in alone, and Tanya and I will be rolling on the floor by the time you make it to the door. Plus ya'll live on the ninth floor and I don't trust that she won't try to throw my ass out the window."

I shook my head knowing she was right.

I heard the elevator ding again. I was sure Amber was on her way up.

"That's the white girl. I saw her pulling up in her little Honda Accord when I was getting out my Mustang," Portia said while blowing a bubble with the gum in her mouth and checking out her nails.

Amber appeared around the corner. She was dressed like a college student wearing grey sweat pants, tennis shoes, and a white t-shirt, with a Hello Kitty on the front. Her brownish-blonde hair was pulled up into a ponytail.

"Hey T, I came as fast as I could," she said.

"We can see that from the looks of your attire," Portia said.

Amber looked at Portia before giving me a funny look and then rolling her eyes.

Here they go.

"Hey Portia, you headed to a video shoot in the hood or something?"

Portia looked at Amber, blew another bubble with her gum, and gave half of a fake smile before she responded.

"I'm not even going to comment on that foolish question. It's not my fault you don't know how to dress. All that money yo' mama and daddy got and you still dress like a fucking broke ass college girl."

"Ha, you call what you have on knowing how to dress? Dressing like a stripper, or some video hoe doesn't make you a fashionista my sista! Ms. I'm-only-hood-rich because of my baby daddy paying out the ass for two kids," Amber challenged.

Damn!

I had to intervene. This was getting ugly and fast.

"Ladies, please, can we stop this before going inside?"

Portia rolled her eyes at Amber and from the look on her face I knew she wanted to respond to her last statement, but thought twice about it.

"Yea, let's hurry up and get this over with I don't have time to go back and forth with amateur wannabe comedians, I have clients to tend to," she said.

"Do any of them still have hair, or are all the horses in Chicago missing their tails?" I heard Amber ask.

I shot Amber a look while trying to cover a laugh. Portia was known as the weave specialist throughout the metro area. I didn't even know what her real hair looked like, or if she even had any hair left.

I walked the ladies in to the apartment and found Tanya seated on the couch wearing a different t-shirt and a pair of leggings. I smelled the Lilac Febreze she had sprayed in the air to cover up what we had done in the kitchen. I said a small prayer before going in behind them.

Terrance

"Are you out of your fucking mind?" Portia screamed at me.

"Watch your mouth in our house," Tanya said.

"Oh go to hell Tanya, you know this shit is ridiculous," Portia said.

Tanya gave her a look. I was taking a big chance on having all three of them in the same room together and expecting them to control their tempers.

I looked around the room. Tanya was shaking her head back and forth and Amber had her mouth open. I had just told them all about the *arrangement.*

I had four children between the three women and I wanted them to grow up in the same house. I was going to purchase one big place and they could all move into it and raise my kids together. It was those family values I was sticking to.

"Let me get this straight. You want us to move into one house, under one roof, with all of your kids, so that we can get a piece of your insurance money, and fulfill your last dying wish? What about our lives and what we want? What do you think people will say about this *arrangement,* as you keep referring to it?" Amber asked.

I paused.

The look on Tanya's face was a bit intimidating. I knew the other two women were very outspoken and would give me their thoughts on the drop of a dime. My wife, on the other hand, was like a brewing storm.

"I don't want my kids to struggle in my ….absence" I couldn't say the word death. "You all know I have taken good care of my kids and all of you …."

Portia cut me off midsentence.

"So continue to take care of them! Leave a check in TJ and Teyah's name, and I'll put it into a trust fund. You know I don't even like these two enough to cohabitate with them, and in my opinion you don't look like your dying to me."

Amber made a noise in agreement. Tanya remained quiet.

"I know this should have been discussed prior to meeting like this, but I came up with this plan while in the hospital, and decided to execute it right away," I argued.

"You call this a plan?" Tanya asked in a voice so low it was scary.

Portia stood up putting both of her hands on her hips.

"You have got to be smoking crack to ask this bullshit of us! Now that I think about it you have lost some weight, and you were sweating and breathing hard when I got off the elevator. You high right now aren't you?" She asked peering at me closely.

"Really Portia?" This woman had lost her mind accusing me of being on crack. *Crack is wack,* as the dearly departed Whitney Houston said.

"Why in the hell would I move my children, and my things, in with the two of them just because that's what you want?" She asked me. I knew she was going to make this difficult.

"Portia, your business at the hair salon is declining and I know you could use the help," I countered.

"What the hell do you know about the business at my shop?" She fired back defensively.

"You must have forgotten who is still paying for the upkeep of that damn shop?" Tanya interjected.

Portia was quiet for a moment. I knew she hated to be reminded that I helped her get her own beauty salon.

"You are a silent partner Terrance. Silent! That means you don't get to say shit about my shop unless asked!"

She grabbed her purse from the couch and began to walk away.

"Where are you going we are not done?" I stood up.

She turned around and shot me an evil look.

"I, Portia Chanel Jackson, am done! You need help! I'm going to call up Dr. Phil, or Oprah, or Maury, or somebody. Hell, even Judge Mathis. This is some bullshit they all need on their show!"

She walked out slamming the door behind her.

When I looked over at Amber, she was twisting a lock of her hair and stopped before she spoke.

"I don't know what to say Terrance. This plan of yours is really outlandish. As much as I hate to say this, Portia is right. How could you think that the three of us could live under one roof and get along?"

She glanced over at Tanya who had her eyes glued to the floor.

"I feel for poor Tanya here. She is your wife and you didn't even give her the respect of discussing it with her first. You haven't changed. Always doing whatever you want and then letting others suffer the consequences."

She rose from her seated position.

"You haven't even let me finish going over the details," I said.

Amber gave a smug laugh and said,

"There is no need for you to finish. I know you. All you are going to try and do next is convince me as to why this *arrangement* is perfect for the kids."

"Exactly," I replied.

"Yes, and that's exactly why I am not staying around to listen to that crap. Goodbye!"

She walked out the door leaving me alone to face my wife.

I looked at Tanya who suddenly sprang to life as if someone had electrocuted her. She jumped up from the couch and started pacing the room.

"All I want to know is why? Why are you doing this to me? How could you come in, make love to me, bring these women to our house, and then drop this bomb on me without warning? Is it not enough that I have had to put up with your baby mama's on every level of mess they have brought over the years? Then you tried to kill yourself, and now you want me to live with them under the same roof? How dare you Terrance? I have been nothing but supportive to you in everything! This right here…..this is on a whole other level of bullshit! What were you thinking? No, I know, you weren't thinking. It's the medication right? Tell me it's the medication they have you on and I'll give you the benefit of the doubt!"

Tanya stopped pacing and collapsed to the floor in tears. My heart sank lower than it ever had before.

"I can't take much more Terrance I just can't," she sobbed.

"Baby, I'm sorry. I never meant for this to hurt you. I just want all of my children to be raised together. You know how I am about family. I don't want my kids growing up separately. That's not how I was raised. My brother and sisters, we were all raised together under one roof. Besides, you know Portia is struggling with that shop. She can't even make her rent payments on her condo."

"Amber's grown ass is living at home with her parents, while trying to take care of my son. Our lease is up on this condo, and there is no point in renewing it with a baby on the way since we need more space. I just want to take care of my kids! I don't know what you women don't understand about that! I don't want to die knowing that they will all suffer in some way."

I paused briefly to gage her reaction, but she would not look at me so I continued.

"If I purchase a big house you can live there rent free having to worry about nothing, but raising my children, and taking care of yourselves."

Tanya started laughing.

"Do you hear yourself? Do you? You sound like a real jack ass. You want your wife, and your two baby mama's in one house! I guess next you are going to ask for a threesome too," she said.

I raised my eyebrows. The thought sounded very appealing, but I didn't mean to show my interest. Tanya read my expression.

"You are a fucking lunatic!"

I started to speak but she raised her hand up in protest.

"Don't you dare say another word to me Terrance McCall Davenport; you have said enough as it is!"

"Tanya, baby, please, try to hear my reasoning."

"Terrance, I said don't say another word to me! Just leave me the hell alone!"

I watched as my wife walked out the room leaving me alone to my thoughts.

Portia

Mama, can we go to the video game store?" TJ asked.

"No baby not today. Mama has some work to do," I said while starting the engine to my car.

"Can I call daddy and ask if he can take me?"My blood started to boil at the mention of his father.

"No! Now sit back and be quiet!" I yelled.

"Mama Tanya never yells at me like that," TJ mumbled.

No he didn't just call this bitch mama.

"What did you just say?"

"I said…"

I popped him in his mouth before he could finish smart mouthing off to me.

TJ crossed his arms and began to pout. I shook my head. His ass was spoiled.

It was Terrance's fault for giving him everything he wanted. I looked in my rearview mirror at my baby Teyah, who was fast asleep in her car seat. She was so quiet, sweet, and innocent the exact opposite of me!

She wasn't even supposed to make it out of my fallopian tubes. As usual Terrance came running to me to clear his head, and like a sucker for love and a big dick, I fell for it again and again. I can't believe he actually came up with that dumb shit, *the arrangement*, as he called it. I should have left his ass alone after my son was born, but he was just so damn fine, and the sex was just too damn good.

I was dick drunk! I let the sex cloud my thinking.

Shaking my head I started drifting off into deep thought again, until the sound of my blackberry ringing in my purse brought me back to reality.

"Hello."

"Is this Portia Jackson?" Some unfamiliar voice asked me.

"Yes, who is this?"

"Ms. Jackson, this is attorney Michael Hopewell. I represent Delilah Fowler."

Oh shit! That was the broad I beat up at my shop two weeks ago for trying to stiff me on my money.

"Okay and how may I help you?" I asked him.

"Ms. Fowler, would like to press charges on you for assault and battery, and is suing you for the damage to her hair. I know it sounds trivial, but this matter can get tied up in small claims court. So that I am not wasting my time or yours, let's say we come to some type of settlement amount," he said.

Is he serious? I am not giving that bitch one red penny of my money!

"Mr. Hope whoever, you can tell Delilah to kiss my ass. I did my job even after I told her getting a perm and then bleaching her hair at the same time would be destructive."

There was silence on the other end. I was sure this jack ass was taking notes of the conversation.

"I see. Well the story Ms. Fowler has given on record is much different. She states that you knew she was sensitive to peroxide, but because you were having a bad day with your child's father, you failed to remember that key point when doing her hair. She also says she tried to remind you several times, but you cut her off and told her to and I quote, "sit your nappy head ass down I will get to you in a minute".

"Ha! That bitch is lying! I didn't tell her anything like that! I treat my clients with the same respect they treat me. She tried to beat me up after she left the shop looking like Whoopi Goldberg instead of Halle Berry. Now here she wants to sue me when I should be the one suing her for tearing up my shop and wasting my time. Don't call me anymore with this shit I will have my attorney contact you."

I hung up on him.

The nerve of that ugly ass heffa trying to bring a claim against me, I should go beat her ass again just for that.

This day was getting better and better. First Terrance asks me to move in with his wife and his other baby mama and now one of my clients wants to sue me.

I need a drink!

I looked at the clock. It was only 11:30a.m. I couldn't wait for happy hour at four. I needed to check my schedule and move some folks around so I could make sure I was the first one there when the bar opened. I dialed up my shop.

"Thank you for calling Classy Sassy Hair how can I help you?" My cousin sang through the phone.

"It's how may I help you, Shavonne! I need you to check my schedule."

"Hey cousin, hold on a minute," she said.

I hired my cousin as my receptionist because she was family, and I didn't trust too many bitches around me. She was a freshman in college, and needed some extra money to pay for her books.

"You have a sew-in at twelve-thirty, a relaxer at two, and a lace front and eyelashes at three," she said.

"Okay, call my three o'clock and see if I can reschedule her to tomorrow morning at nine. Is there any mail?" I inquired.

"Yup the usual, bills, supply orders, oh and a letter from some insurance company."

"Oh shit, I forgot to pay the premium again this month. Wait how do you know? Shavonne, are you reading my mail again?" I asked.

"Why yes, cousin that's what you pay me to do. Answer phones, open mail, make orders, and take appointments," she responded.

"Put my mail back in the envelope and reseal it until I get there!" I never asked her to open my mail. This girl was giving me a headache.

"Okay if that's what you want me to do. Do you think you can tighten up my weave for me? I want to look fly for the R. Kelly concert this weekend."

The pain in my head started to throb slowly. I could hear her voice but didn't want to acknowledge it. I needed a drink bad.

"Cousin, are you still there? Did you hear what I asked you?" She said this time louder.

"Dammit Shavonne yes I heard you! Just know that I'm going to deduct that from your pay."

Before she could protest I hung up on her.

I dropped the kids off at daycare, took a sip of the warm vodka out of my silver flask I carried in my purse, and waited for the throbbing in my head to stop. Once the liquor kicked in I headed in to start my day at work praying that nothing else would go wrong before three pm.

Amber

"Are you telling me he can do this Rebecca?"

I was on the phone with my attorney and best friend, Rebecca Smith.

"Yes Amber, he can put stipulations on the disbursement of his settlement money and this one is attached to his last will & testament," she replied.

"I don't have to agree to this!   Becky you know this is stupid."

I just couldn't get over what Terrance wanted me to do.

"I told him it was stupid, but he wasn't trying to hear me. From reading this it doesn't sound too bad," Rebecca said.

Is she serious right now?

Terrance had her send all of us a letter outlining all the details he tried to discuss with us.

"You can't be serious! Did you see that he is asking me to move in with Portia and his wife Tanya?" I asked her.

"Yes I seen that, but look at what it says in the following paragraph,"

She began to reread it to me.

"This arrangement is in the interest and protection of the children that will be left behind in the event of my death. All said children mentioned are under the age of 18 and are unable to care for themselves leaving complete care to their mothers. I am providing them all with substantial amounts of money to cover the cost of their life expenses. To my eldest son, Nathan McCall Davenport, who is thirteen years in age, I will provide the amount in the sum of 25 million dollars to be paid out to his mother, Amber Sykowski, with the exception she agrees to the living arrangement described below...."

I had a bad taste in my mouth. Lord knows I needed the money, so I wouldn't have to depend on my parents anymore, but I did not feel it was worth compromising my sanity to get it.

"It is in the interest of the children. If he buys one of those really big houses you could get one wing of the house and not have to see the other two mothers."

She laughed and I just shook my head.

"Rebecca, you don't have any idea who the other two mothers are," I told her.

"Correction, I know who Tanya is, she went to the same high school as we did. She was quiet back then and I'm sure she can't be all that bad now," Rebecca said.

Tanya really wasn't a problem. She and I got along for the most part. I respected her because she respected me, but I had to admit I was jealous that she had what I wanted and could have had. Terrance obviously saw something in her that made him want to give her his last name. I was still trying to figure out what that *something* was.

"Well that other one, Portia is crazy. She purposely set Terrance up to have his two children," I reminded her.

Rebecca laughed again which was becoming really annoying.

"You set him up too remember? I was the one dealing with your pregnant ass while he was away in college. I was also with you that night after senior prom when you purposely poked holes in the condoms; because you knew he was headed to the NBA."

This chic was nuts.

"What? My son was conceived in love not bribery. I didn't poke holes in that damn thing. I barely knew how to use them. I was only seventeen," I reminded her.

"Okay Amber if you say so. You still haven't faced reality," she said.

"Reality of..?"

"You still love Terrance."

"No the hell I don't. We have a thirteen year old son together that's as far as my love goes."

"Well why haven't you moved on in all these years and found anyone else to be with?"

I really could not answer her question.

"I have to go pick up Nathan from school." I needed to get off this phone.

"You didn't answer my question Amber."

"Becky, I don't have time for this right now. I'll call you later," I said to her.

"I bet you could hire a driver with that money to drive you around in your own limo," she kept talking.

"You must be smoking whatever Terrance is smoking," I said.

"I'm just saying let this man take care of you and his child. So what if it's two other broads involved. At least Nate will get to grow up with his brothers and sister."

That was it. I have had it with her jokes.

"Goodbye Rebecca!"

I hung up the phone while hearing her laughing in the background.

She didn't know me like that. Sure we been friends for over ten years, but she still doesn't know me like she thinks she does. I couldn't believe she said I set Terrance up to have a baby with me. That was a lie. What I needed to do was get a life of my own and move away from Chicago.

I had no type of love life living at home with my parents, because I preferred dating black men. That factor alone made my mother's skin crawl. She had to accept Nathan because he was her only grandchild, but she surely didn't want to accept anyone else.

As I grabbed my keys to walk out the door my cell phone rang. I thought it was Rebecca calling to pick with me some more. Without looking at the caller ID I answered it and gave her a piece of my mind,

"Look bitch the shit isn't funny so you can keep laughing all you want to and making a mockery of this shit."

There was silence.

"Uhhh hello …..Amber? This is Tanya..."

I felt stupid.

"Oh sorry Tanya I thought you were someone else..What's up?"

"Maybe I should be asking you what's up, but I have a feeling I already know. Anyway, Terrance is starting to get sicker and he is asking to see Nathan. I honestly doubt he will make it the six months he is telling everyone. I thought about throwing him an early birthday party on Saturday and having it just between the kids and a few friends you know…something happy."

She paused.

"I'm game. Do you need me to bring anything?" I asked.

"No. I will email you the directions to the place."

"The place?"

"Yes girl, Terrance may be sick, but he's still trying to push this *arrangement* on us. He rented the house he is thinking about buying, and wants me to hold the party there. He feels if we see it we might fall in love with it," Tanya said.

A noise of detest escaped my lips before I could catch it.

Tanya laughed.

"Trust me I feel the same way, but I'm too tired to argue with him about this mess anymore," she said.

There was silence as I thought of what to say next.

"Tanya, how are you holding up?" I asked.

"Most days I'm okay and others I'm not. Thanks for asking."

"No problem."

"Listen Amber I'm not going to keep you. If you and Nate can make it, it's going to be next Saturday at noon."

"Okay thanks Tanya take care of yourself and we'll see ya then."

I closed my cell phone and felt an instant sadness. Here we are worried about living together and how our kids would manage being without their father, when Tanya is the one pregnant, and trying to deal with how to be without her husband. I could only imagine the pain she was feeling knowing any moment he would be gone and she would be alone. I shook off the chill that instantly came over me and headed outside to my car.

Terrance

My health is deteriorating! I am feeling weak and the pain in my chest is becoming unbearable. Since my wife can't possibly do all of this on her own anymore, here I sit laid up in this hospital bed hooked up to all these machines. All type of pain medicine is running through my veins. Chemotherapy works, but only for a short period of time then the pain comes right back. All the hair on my head is pretty much gone, so I had Tanya shave me bald. The pain in my chest feels like a ton of bricks crushing inside of me. I wish I had a choice. I would choose life. I would ask for the cancer to die and let me live. I would ask God for one more chance.

I would go back and undo all the hurt and pain I caused my wife and the women who had my children. I watch my wife as she moves around the house trying her best to stay strong under the circumstances. She doesn't know, but I hear her crying at night when she thinks I'm sleep. The sound of her tears feel like stabs from a knife directly hitting my heart. I think about my two boys and how they look like me. It hurts to know I won't be around to teach them how to tie a tie, or how to spit game to a woman. I can't even throw a football or basketball around with them, or be able to show them how to change the oil in a car. These are things in life a man should know that my dad taught me, but I am not going to be able to show my boys! I won't be able to walk my only daughter down the aisle if she ever was to get married, or warn her about guys like me when I was younger.

This shit hurts!

I knocked over the tray on the side of my bed sending it crashing to the floor. My nurse came running through the door.

"Terrance, is everything alright?"

I looked at the long haired, Mexican nurse standing in my room. She was beautiful. Her face was void of any makeup showing her natural beauty.

"Nurse Lynn, are you married?" I asked. I was hoping she would do me a favor and give me another hand job. Maybe I would get lucky and she would put her mouth on it this time. I wasn't sure if I had any life left in my dick, but whatever little bit I had I was going to use.

I could see her cheeks flush with color.

"No I am not. Why do you ask?"

She picked the tray up from the floor and placed it back on the bedside table. Her ass wasn't big like Tanya's or Portia's, but it was a nice heart shape.

"You are beautiful! Any man would be lucky to be married to you." I waited to see if my dick would salute so that she would feel sorry for me.

She smiled. I felt a slight buldge underneath my hospital gown.

"Still charming the ladies I see," my guy Jason said.

There goes my blow job.

He must have come through the door when I was looking at the nurse.

"I'll leave you two alone," she said before walking away.

Jason and I had been childhood friends for over sixteen years. We went to the same junior high, high school and college together. He stayed in Atlanta and I moved back home to Chicago after school was done.

"Jason, my man, what are you doing here?"

He leaned in and gave me a handshake and a half shoulder hug. When we pulled apart, his face took on a different expression.

"I was in town on business and I ran into Tanya at the grocery store. She broke down and told me everything."

He pulled up a chair next to my bed.

"Why didn't you call and tell me man? You know I would have come back home right away."

"How do you call up your best friend and tell him.....you are dying!"

The room was quiet. I fought back the tears.

"Do you know how hard it was telling Tanya that shit? The doctor visits, the chemotherapy sessions, the hair loss, the rashes, the vomiting. Man, I haven't made love to my wife in months! I can't even stay awake long enough to get an erection! This shit is fucked up!"

Jason just shook his head and gave me that look I was accustomed to seeing on everyone's face.

Pity!

"Dawg, I don't know what to say. I'm not used to seeing you like this. You know you used to always be *the man*! Seeing you laid up here with all these tubes knowing that one day tomorrow may never come for you…..." he trailed off. "How are my God children doing? Are there any more I should know about?"

We both gave a small laugh.

"No there's no more to my knowledge. Knowing Portia's ass she probably pregnant right now and telling everyone it's mine," I replied.

He shook his head.

"Portia Jackson! I'm still trying to figure that shit out! How in the hell did you have any kids with that tramp? You know everybody and they daddy slept with that hoe in Chicago, Milwaukee, Gary, everywhere. Those kids probably aren't your kids."

I couldn't do anything but laugh and shake my head.

He better be kidding about that shit!

"Man, she had that G-A-P!"

He looked at me before smiling.

"That good -ass -pussy," we both said at the same time giving each other pound.

"You know that will get a brother caught up every time!" I said.

"What will get you caught up every time?" Tanya said coming through the door.

"Not seeing my beautiful wife on a daily basis," I said.

Tanya looked refreshed. Her eyes weren't as puffy and she had a type of glow surrounding her as if she had renewed her faith in life somehow. I felt my disease had spread to her emotionally killing off the beauty I had grown to love.

I watched as Tanya gave Jason a hug and how comfortable they seemed together. In the back of my mind I wondered if they had ever been together behind my back. Tanya would be justified if she did sleep with my best friend.

In the past I took advantage of her kindness and naiveté, and gave her the business where other women were concerned. I still remember the day she came home from the doctor after finding out she was pregnant.

****

"Terrance, we need to talk."

"It has to wait; I am running late I have to get to the site in 30 minutes."

"No, we need to talk now!" Tanya yelled at me.

"Tanya I don't have time for this bullshit."

"So having a baby is bullshit?"

I stopped dead in my tracks almost burning myself with the coffee I had in my cup.

"Having a baby? What the hell do that have to do with....wait, are you pregnant?"

I expected her to be excited since this would be her first child, but the reaction I received was so cold.

"I guess I am. I also have gonorrhea."

This time I did burn myself spilling my coffee on the front of my shirt.

"Damn! I have to change my shirt."

"Terrance, are you still messing with Portia?"

At this time Portia and Amber both had a child by me while my own wife didn't have any. Portia and I would mess around from time to time, but for the most part I strapped up.

Sometimes!

"No I am not. How do you know you have it? I don't have any symptoms."

I ducked when she threw the first pot.

"How in the hell can you stand here in my face once again and lie to me! I saw your papers from the free clinic. What kind of sorry ass man are you? You allow me to catch a virus that could not only harm me, but now my fetus and you didn't have the balls to man up and tell me about it?"

Pan number two flew past my head just barely missing me.

"Tanya, stop throwing shit!" I ducked a stock pot this time that hit the floor with a loud clang. "We can talk about this okay? It had to be the last time I was with Portia before the baby was born."

I lied.

Tanya pulled out a knife and ran towards me at a speed that had to be backed by her adrenaline and anger. Even though I was 6'4 and quick on my feet dodging an angry woman with a knife was hard as hell. She cut me on the side of my waist, my arm and she would have succeeded in stabbing me in my thigh had I not moved. I never pressed charges because it was my fault. I had caused her a great deal of pain. A woman in pain is like a loaded gun ready to go off whenever the trigger is pulled.

A smile came across my face as I rubbed the small scar from the cut on my arm after recalling the memory. I looked over at Jason and Tanya and they were still laughing it up about old times. While looking at them I felt a deep unsettling pain forming in the pit of my chest. I knew my time wasn't long. Breathing for me was becoming a painful chore. Tanya could sense my pain when she looked at me. She came close to the bed, touching my hand.

"Terrance, do I need to call the nurse?"

I shook my head and moved my hands to her stomach. I closed my eyes trying to fight the pain. I knew Jason was quiet because he felt helpless not knowing what to say or do. He touched my shoulder and for the first time I saw a tear slip down his cheek.

"Hang in there bro, it's not time yet," he said.

I tried to take a breath despite the excruciating pain hoping he was right.

Tanya

Lord, please forgive me for the feelings I am having right now. Seeing Jason again brings back a flood of memories I thought I had left behind. Jason was Terrance's right hand man. He was his best man in our courthouse wedding and we made him the Godfather of our unborn son.

He let me stay with him when I first found out about Terrance's second child with Portia. I had no intention of having sex with him at that time, but it happened. I felt it was my sweet revenge only I never told Terrance about it. Here I am thinking about it again as my dying husband lies in this hospital bed. Jason must have felt it too. When the nurse came in to give Terrance more morphine, Jason led me close to the door.

"Hey Tanya, you want some coffee?" he quietly asked.

I looked over at Terrance who was now peacefully sleeping. I had to make sure his chest was still moving letting me know he was still alive. The pain medication must have finally kicked in.

"No, I'm alright," I whispered.

Jason smiled at me giving me a feeling inside I thought was gone.

"You always were a strong woman. I admire you for that."

He touched my hand and squeezed it.

I felt like I was going to wet my panties. It had been a long time since Terrance touched me intimately. The medicine kept him sleepy, or he was in too much pain to even think about sex. I didn't realize I had closed my eyes until I heard Jason speak again.

"Tanya?"

"Huh…oh sorry I'm so tired. I haven't gotten much sleep lately. I been running Terrance back and forth from the hospital, to his chemo sessions, and back home, and being pregnant is exhausting. It's just been overwhelming to say the least."

He held on to my hand. I almost felt guilty for not wanting to let it go.

"Hey listen why don't I drive you home and I'll stay up here for the night. I don't have to be back in Atlanta until next week Wednesday," he offered.

"Jason thanks, but I couldn't ask that of you."

"You aren't asking me I'm offering it."

A tear slipped down my cheek. My emotions were so out of sort that it seemed all I did lately was cry. Jason grabbed me, pulling me into a tight embrace. His arms were warm. He held on to me with such care and concern that I just sobbed in his arms.

"You want me to take you home?" He asked.

I looked back at Terrance not really wanting to leave his side.

"Just to grab a change of clothes, I want to be here for every moment," I said. He nodded his head in understanding.

He escorted me to my car and drove me home. There was silence between us as he drove while still holding on to my hand. He held my hand as we got out of the car and walked over to the elevator. I pulled out my key card to activate the elevator and we stood there in silence, holding hands. When the elevator door opened, my neighbor Ms. Lee stepped off, looked at our hands, and shook her head. She stood there staring at me as if she could see right through me. I prayed for the doors to hurry up and close. It was at that moment I felt guilty.

After unlocking the door to the apartment I shared with Terrance, I stepped inside the foyer flipping on the nearest light switch on the table. I walked into the massive living room staring at the pictures of Terrance and I on the mantle, and the chocolate, Italian leather sectional we had picked out together. I knew I didn't want to stay here by myself. There were too many memories. When I turned around and looked at Jason, he was watching me with a look in his eyes that I had seen before in Terrance's. It was one of desire and lust. I felt a tingling sensation below my waist as he looked at me. My hands went to my bulging belly out of habit.

"Tanya, you are one beautiful pregnant woman do you know that?"

"Um I suppose if toting around a gut full of human is cute then that's me."

I smiled and tried to laugh to break the sexual tension that seemed to fill the air.

Jason came and stood over me. He was the same height as Terrance. Before I knew what was happening I put my arms around his waist and my head rested against his chest. He pulled me into an embrace and held me.

"Terrance used to hold me just like this."

I felt tears coming to my eyes once again.

Jason lifted up my chin and kissed my lips softly. A moan escaped my lips.

"Jason please, don't do this," I begged.

"Don't do what? We have done this before."

He kissed me again this time forcing his tongue inside my mouth. His kiss tasted like minty fresh gum. I don't know what took over, but I found myself trying desperately to inhale him. He didn't stop me but returned the passion equally. Our tongues intertwined as if they were dancing a rhythm only we knew. I felt his hand on my breast as he slipped it underneath my t-shirt. I was a bit embarrassed I didn't have on better clothing. Lately, the hospital trips had me in sweat pants and a t-shirt.

He rubbed my nipple between his thumb and forefinger sending chills down my spine. Being pregnant made me even more sensitive to the touch.

Jason picked me up and carried me to the couch in the living room. I was impressed by his ability to carry me even though I was five months pregnant. He pulled my sweat pants off in one fluid motion.

I need to stop him.

He proceeded to lift his polo shirt over his head revealing a chiseled body that had spent hours in the gym. He was perfect in every sense. He removed my panties tossing them to the floor as he placed his head in between my thighs and began to lick my other pair of lips with gentle flicks of his tongue.

Stop him you are carrying Terrance's baby this isn't right.

My conscience was screaming at me. I knew I should have stopped him but the feeling was extremely hard to fight.

"I'll take care of you," he said. "When Terrance dies you won't have to worry about a thing. I'll be your man." He continued to lick.

What?

"You need someone to take care of you who won't take advantage of you and your son when ya'll inherit all that money." He continued to lick.

Wait how did he know about the money?

The flickering of his tongue became harder as my body betrayed me and caused me to moan and shake. I closed my eyes as the tears slipped down my cheeks. It was a euphoric feeling. It wasn't long before the waves of pleasure I was receiving took completely over.

"Oh God Terrance," I cried out.

I felt Jason's body tense and pause for a brief second before he continued. Visions of Terrance making love to me in the kitchen just a few months ago were in my head. I felt Jason, but I saw Terrance. It was surreal. Jason brought me to a place I hadn't seen in a long time. Right at the peak of my orgasm I started crying and carrying on so much that Jason tried to stop, but I locked my thighs around his head and held him there. The pain of losing Terrance before he was gone was taking over me. After what seemed like forever but was only a few minutes, I opened my eyes to look at Jason. He had tears in his eyes as he wiped his face. The area around his mouth glistened from my love juice.

"Tanya, I am so sorry I don't know what came over me. I guess seeing you after all this time and knowing that...."

I touched his hand so that he wouldn't say what I already knew he was going to.

"It's okay Jason really. I got caught up too."

I was embarrassed when my baby started to kick. Jason noticed.

"Wow little man is mad at me." A panic looked crossed his face. "You aren't going to tell…Terrance are you?"

I shook my head. My husband may be dying but I wasn't trying to kill him no sooner than he was supposed to go. I heard the sound of the floor creaking and when I looked up towards the door I realized I forgot to close it. Jason got up to use the bathroom and when I went to shut the door the person standing in front of it made me lose my breath. She was watching us.

Portia

Sipping on my fourth glass of Carlos Rossi Rhine I was feeling good and tipsy. The past month had been a living hell. Terrance was dying, my client was suing me, and my shop was going into foreclosure, and I was damn near broke. My friends stopped coming around and I haven't had a good man in my life in a long ass time. Terrance was always my go to for a good back breaking sex session. He had the type of dick that could set your entire body aflame and leave you burning with lust and desire. He could make a girl scream just by touch alone.

I sure could use one of those hot and sweaty sessions right about now!

Tanya is one lucky bitch to have that type of man in her bed every night. I know I sound stupid settling for the pieces of him he gave to me, but I loved him.

I love him!

Damn!

I love him still even after all these years!

I know I'm drunk now because I just admitted that shit out loud to myself.

I had no intention of driving to Terrance's house. I have no idea how I got there. I saw Tanya's black BMW pull into the underground garage as I was sitting outside and wanted to talk to her. I was a fool to think that she would open up the door willingly and talk to me.

I was able to get in the building through the front door when the little bitty old lady coming out of it forgot to close it. I had almost made it to the elevator until the damn building security noticed me and stopped me.

"Excuse me miss are you here to visit someone?" He asked.

"Hey there…." I read his name badge "Allen….I left my car keys in my baby daddy's apartment and I have to come get them from his wife, so that's what I'm doing." My words sounded a bit slurred, but I tried to keep it together.

The security guard gave me the once over while stopping his eyes on my breasts. I picked the wrong time to wear a push up bra.

"Well I'll let you up if you let me get a peek." He nodded his head towards my breasts. I could see why the only job he could get was doing security. He was obese, ugly, and looked like a very bad version of Biggie Smalls.

I shook my head. It was always the fat ones who wanted something from me. All I had to do was flash a titty and let him touch my ass, and after one minute he made a mess of his pants and activated the elevator with his key for me.

Walking down the hallway towards Terrance's apartment, I could hear what sounded like a cat in heat. I had to slip off my heels, and walk barefoot, because the effects of the alcohol had me almost break my neck. When I got to the correct loft, the door was slightly ajar inviting my curiosity inside. I could hear what sounded like moans of pleasure.

I was anxious to see if it was Terrance giving Tanya a final goodbye, something I knew I would never get. When I peeked inside I noticed a very tall and very fine ass light-skinned brother that wasn't Terrance, tonguing down Tanya's pregnant pussy right on her couch. Her head was thrown back and her eyes were rolling in the back of her head.

Damn, even while pregnant this bitch still gets all the action.

I was jealous.

I stepped inside the hallway of the apartment and tried to close the door quietly behind me. I don't know why I didn't just turn around and leave. I suppose it was the voyeur in me. I needed to see who it was Tanya was cheating on Terrance with. When he finally showed his face I realized it was Terrance's best friend, Jason.

Ain't that something!

Out of all the people in the world, she chose her husband's best friend. This was going to be good. Lucky bitch!

I can't stand her. Wait until I tell Terrance about this shit!

I took the last swallow out of my bottle I had carried with me and threw it back in my Chanel bag. I had to get out of there. I made a move for the door but the damn floorboard I stepped on made a creaky noise. I saw Tanya move from the couch out the corner of my eye and I did my best to slip through the door. She made it to the entrance before I could make it out and I had no choice, but to turn around and scare her pregnant ass. So I stood there.

I knew I had scared her because her breath caught in her throat and she looked like she had seen a ghost. I had no words to say to her, but I let her know I had seen her just by looking at her.

Before she could say anything, I turned on my heels and ran down to the elevator. I knew I was too drunk to drive, but I sure as hell wasn't going to stay in that nasty bitch's house.

When I was pregnant I never let another man touch me. I had to get home. The elevator was taking too long to come. I watched down the hall for Tanya. A sense of relief swept over me when I heard the bell alerting me the doors were about to open. Once I arrived to the first floor, instead of going through the front door and running into the horny security guard again, I slipped out the side door. My car was still parked out front. I jumped in, threw my shoes in the backseat and skirted off. The road was blurry and the streetlights looked like they were dancing. I thought I saw someone cross in front of me, so I slammed on my brakes, hit the curb, and spun my Mustang right into a utility pole.

Amber

It was Saturday, the day of Terrance's party. I had just logged off my laptop after receiving pictures of the house that Terrance was going to purchase. It was a beautiful home. It had seven bedrooms, six bathrooms, an outdoor pool, six car garage, basketball court, computer and study room. The closets were huge. It reminded me of the closet Carrie Bradshaw had in that movie, Sex and the City.

I could tell Terrance specifically went through every room of the house making sure there was something in each room that would appeal to all of us.

Since we were all women he made sure the closet space was large enough for our clothes. I had to give it to him the brother was on point with everything. We wouldn't have to worry about a thing.

When I really thought about it, living under the same roof as Portia was just not in the cards for my life. That girl brought more drama and mayhem to herself than anyone else I knew.

I heard recently she had went by Terrance's house all drunk and then crashed into a pole. She came out without a scratch but more crap to complain about.

"Nathan, are you ready to go?" I shouted.

"Yea, ma."

My son came into the room wearing basketball shorts; a white t-shirt, and Adidas flip flops. He looked just like Terrance did when he was in college.

"We are not going to play basketball. Don't you think you could have put on a pair of jeans?"

"Mom, this is comfortable and besides dad is too sick to care about what I have on."

I guess he had a point.

I looked over my own attire and felt a bit underdressed. I had on a pair of jeans from Abercrombie and an Aeropostale t-shirt. I wasn't one for dressing up.

Nathan left the room to change his clothes and this time came back dressed like a mini rapper wearing a blue hat, sagging jeans, a white t-shirt and a pair of name brand shoes his father had bought him. His I-pod was on his hip, along with his I-phone and he had his earphones in his ears. A big silver cross hung from his neck. I looked him over and was about to make a comment about his choice of attire when my mother came waltzing into the room.

"Where are you two off to?" She asked.

"To a birthday party mom," I answered.

"Whose?"

"A party Nathan was invited to."

"Okay so whose party is it?" She asked again.

I sighed. My mother really worked my nerves. She always had to know my movements and whereabouts, and who I was taking my child around as if I wasn't grown.

"It's Nathan's family."

I watched my mother turn her face up like she smelled something bad.

"You are a good one. I wouldn't be taking my child around those... people."

"What people mama? You don't even know them." I started gathering my things.

"I know Terrance and that alone is enough."

I grabbed my purse and the keys to my car to head out the door. Maybe if I ignored her she would stop talking. I was wrong.

"You going to parade around at a party with your child like you were proud to be this man's whore. He didn't even have the respect to make you his wife and you know why? They only use *us* white women for our credit, status, and pleasure. None of *them* can afford anything on their own. Then, *they* make all these mixed breed babies, so *they* can have decent looking children without nappy hair."

"Mama!" I was appalled at what she said.

I was hoping Nathan had his music on, but from the look on his face I could tell he heard what she said. Quickly, I pushed Nathan out the door before he had to be subjected to anything else that came out of her mouth.

I can't believe she called me Terrance's whore.

Tears came to my eyes at the thought of my mother viewing me in such a low status. I couldn't understand what her problem was. I deserved love just like any other woman no matter if the man was black, white, green, or blue. I shook off all the things my mother said and drove off.

The drive to the house located in Highland Park, Illinois was about forty minutes. When I followed the directions Tanya gave, I was surprised to drive by Michael Jordan's house that was up for sale. Terrance surely had gone all out to get a house in this location.

Pulling up to the circular driveway, the house was huge and looked even better in person than it did in the pictures. There was a valet attendant that greeted me and offered to park my car. Upon entering the huge double doors, a maid with a tray, handed me some type of cocktail drink and gave a soda to Nathan. Another woman who I assumed was the hostess directed me to the back yard where everyone was located. Upon stepping out on the massive patio and from the look of the decorations, Tanya went all out. She had a bounce house for the kids; lots of carnival games, pony rides, an arcade room, a make-your-own funnel cake station, and what looked like millions of blue and red balloons everywhere. The pool had floating candles and someone was walking around in a clown costume entertaining the children.

There were several people carrying silver trays passing out hor d'oeuvres, glasses of champagne for the adults, and cute glasses of soda for the kids.

Nathan immediately headed to the arcade room.

I noticed Jason standing by the pool and decided to speak.

"Hey Jason how are you?"

He turned and looked at me with a big smile.

"Hey Amber, long time no see. You are looking good as usual. Is that my Godson Nate I saw walk over there? Damn, he looks like a light skinned Terrance."

We both were quiet for a minute until Portia's loud mouth interrupted us.

"I see Terrance is laying it on extra thick by bringing us out here to this mini mansion. What made her pick a carnival theme? It just looks tacky," she said. "Look at this pool. All that stuff she got floating around in it. She should have hired a real decorator."

Portia smelled and looked like she had just come back from happy hour. She had on shiny gold leggings, a cream colored off the shoulder sweater, big gold hoop earrings, and a gold Dolce & Gabbana clutch. She almost made me ashamed of my casual attire. I assumed her stilettos had to be some brand name designer from the way she was strutting around in them.

"Hey Portia," Jason said.

Portia looked at him and then back at me.

"Well look who we have here. It's the tongue Casanova."

Portia grabbed a champagne glass from one of the trays that was passing by. I watched as she took a gulp instead of a sip.

Jason frowned and looked at me confused.

We both watched as she downed the champagne in record time.

"Are you trying to score Amber next?" She asked Jason. She set her empty glass down in a nearby plant and grabbed another glass from another tray being carried by.

"Now this is some good wine here," Portia said gulping down her second glass just like the first.

"Portia, just what the hell is a tongue Casanova?" Jason asked her.

"Maybe, I should get in line and see what all the fuss is about. See what you can do with that tongue of yours," she said in a not so hushed tone.

"Maybe, you should stop drinking, all that alcohol is going to your head," he suggested.

I too was curious as to what she was talking about, but before I could ask her to elaborate, a very frail and weak looking Terrance was wheeled outside in a wheelchair to be amidst the activities. Teyah, Nathan, and Terrance Jr. ran up to their father and gave him a hug. Everyone had to stop because it truly was a perfect moment.

Portia smacked her lips and took another gulp.

"He is the picture perfect fucking father. I need another drink! Do they have real alcohol up in here?" Portia asked.

I handed her my glass of what tasted like a vodka and cranberry juice cocktail.

"Seems like you have had enough to drink for everyone in this party," Jason said.

She took the drink from me and gave Jason the evil eye.

Tanya walked over to where we were standing. She had on a very cute red maternity shirt, with black leggings. Her hair was curly all over and she had on makeup.

"Hey Amber and Jason thanks for coming," She glanced over at Portia.

"Portia," she said all too quickly.

"Hey Kool-Aid," Portia yelled out. "Just kidding I regret saying this, but you actually look cute pregnant. Doesn't she Jason?" Jason frowned at Portia and Tanya nervously looked away.

There was definitely something going on.

"This is a nice party, but I think you could have done better with the decorations," Portia said. The effects of the alcohol had definitely caught up to her. I hadn't noticed that she finished the alcohol in the glass I had given her and was now sucking on the ice cubes.

Jason and I waited on Tanya's response.

"What's wrong with the decorations?" Tanya asked. The same waiter from earlier came back our way carrying a new tray of drinks and Portia reached out to grab another glass. This time Jason snatched it from her and sipped from it before she could say anything. She glared at him.

"A carnival theme, come on Tanya you have money and lots of it! There should have been ice sculptures, circus animals, and people on them stilt things walking around.

Hell, where is the fucking DJ? This isn't a party if there isn't any music. Can't nobody twerk in silence," Portia said.

I stepped in between Tanya and Portia when I saw Tanya move closer.

"Tanya, the decorations are nice. I'm sure Terrance loves it and that's all that matters," I said trying to keep the situation calm.

"Thank you Amber. I'm glad some people appreciate class and not trash. Does anybody smell that?" She sniffed the air. "It smells like cheap alcohol, Portia is that you?"

"If it's that cheap ass watered down shit you passing around on them trays, then I guess it is me. I need to go to the bar and get a real drink," Portia responded.

Jason laughed and pulled Portia away to the inside of the house before Tanya could come up with a comeback.

Tanya shook her head at me and walked off. I looked around the massive back yard at all of the kids playing, and the adults talking. Terrance was in the center of the patio watching everything. I saw a tear slip from his eye. I decided to make my way over to him.

"Hey Terrance what's up?"

"Hey Amber, how are you?"

"I'm good."

My words were stuck in my mouth as I tried to find something else to talk about. Terrance and I really never spoke about much of anything besides Nathan.

"I just wanted to say thank you!" He said.

I wasn't sure why every time he saw me he felt the need to thank me. I assumed it was for bringing Nathan to the party.

"You don't have to thank me. He is your son he deserves to be here," I replied.

Terrance grabbed my hand into his.

"That's not why I am thanking you. Thank you for being a good mother to my son despite your mother and her issues she has with me. I feel good knowing he will be properly cared for in my …absence."

I didn't know what to do or say. Tears were beginning to well up in my eyes.

"It's okay. Nathan brought light to my world. Having him gave me a reason to live."

Just when Terrance was getting ready to speak something happened. His eyes began to roll in the back of his head and his face started turning blue.

The grip on my hand tightened as I felt him trying to fight to breathe. I screamed not knowing what to do. Tanya, Jason, Portia and others came running over. I could see some of the guests trying to gather the children inside the house, so they would not witness what was going on. Terrance's nurse ran over to join us with her stethoscope. She quickly placed it to his chest.

"It sounds like one of his lungs has collapsed he needs to go to the hospital right now!"

From the corner of my eye I could see Nathan in the doorway of the pool house. When I turned around to look at him I saw tears in my son's eyes for the first time. I had kept him sheltered from a lot of things concerning his father, so that he would feel no pain. He had been watching the entire time. I ran over to him.

"Come on honey let's go inside and see what type of food they have." I pulled him over to the table with the food on it.

"I'm not hungry," he said.

"You should try to eat something," I offered.

"I'm not hungry! Is dad going to be okay?" Nathan asked.

I couldn't say anything.

"He is going to die isn't he?" My son looked at me for an answer.

"Yup," Portia said nonchalantly as she took a sip from the plastic cup in her hand. I assumed it was more alcohol she was consuming. I knocked the cup out of her hand tired of her antics.

"I am so sick of you! Do you even give a hell about how this is going to affect *your* children?"

Her nasty ass let out a loud burp before she responded.

"Yes, white bitch I do!" She said slurring her words.

"Who in the hell are you calling a white bitch?" I knew she was drunk but she had more than offended me.

"Ladies, come on don't do this here," Jason said trying to intervene.

"Shut up Jason," I said.

Tanya walked back over to where we were standing.

"Is there a problem here?" She asked.

"Oh it's about to be. She just called me a white bitch."

I took my earrings out of my ears.

"Amber, don't," Jason said trying to intervene again.

"Jason, fuck off. Everybody is always so scared to say or do anything to her and I am not the one."

"Oooo this white girl thinks she got balls! Just because you had a baby by a black man doesn't make you no better than me, boo! You still just a baby mama just like me," Portia said.

I couldn't take it anymore. I walked right up to Portia and punched her in the mouth sending her ass crashing into one of the tables. Next thing I knew it was a girl fight.

Portia jumped up and knocked me down to the floor. She was dripping blood from her mouth on my shirt as we tousled back and forth knocking into things.

"Stop it!" Tanya yelled holding her belly.

Jason and another guest finally were able to pull us apart. Too many years of built up animosity for her came out at the wrong time. The look on Tanya's face was one of disgust and I instantly felt bad for reacting the way I did. Some of the guests began to leave. I searched around for Nathan, but didn't see him. Portia was being escorted out the yard by Jason.

"Don't ever put your hands on me again! You better be glad my children are with me otherwise I would have mopped the floor with your white ass", She screamed at me.

"I'm not scared!" I replied.

Jason quickly moved her away from me before anything else could be said or done. I saw tears streaming down Tanya's cheeks as I approached her to apologize. Before I could get a word in she threw up her hand in protest.

"Don't apologize to me for that. I would have hit her too. I am just saddened that these kids have to continuously see the crap we are dealing with. It hurts. Do you know Terrance doesn't want to go to the hospital? He'd rather sit and die in front of us. I think that is the most selfish thing I have ever heard."

I tried to speak again but she stopped me.

"Don't mind me. I'm a ball of emotions. I'm pregnant and I wanted to sleep with Jason. Make sure Nathan gets a bag of candy before you guys leave."

She walked away from me.

Tanya wants to sleep with Jason? What the hell? Why did she just confess that to me? All I could do was shake my head. Terrance's illness was affecting us all in more ways than one.

I searched the house for Nathan but couldn't find him. I saw Jason come back in the door. He read the look on my face.

"Amber, you alright, did you find Nate?"

I shook my head.

"Don't worry he couldn't of gone too far. I'm sure he is just checking out the house."

After two hours passed by we began to search for him. We searched every square inch of the house. I looked in every closet, bathroom, and every room with no sign of him. After five hours of waiting, panic set in. It was now ten o' clock and dark outside.

"Amber, do you think we need to call your …mother?" Jason asked.

"Hell no! If she finds out her grandson is missing it will be an all-out attack on Terrance. She will swear he had something to do with it," Tanya said.

Tanya was right if my mother got any word of this all hell would break loose.

"No let's just keep looking and calling his cell phone. I'm sure he was just upset and went for a walk," I replied.

I didn't believe my own words. Nathan never got upset. He was a good kid. He got straight A's in school and stayed on the honor roll. He never gave me any problems.

I walked the perimeter of the house while Jason and Tanya walked down the block and back. Jason even got in his car to search the neighborhood and we didn't find him.

Six hours later I was a ball of nerves. The three remaining guest decided to leave, leaving me alone with Jason and Tanya.

"I have no idea where he could be. You don't think he fell in the lake do you? Oh my God he can't swim. I knew I should have gotten him those swim lessons when he was five like Terrance suggested."

I was losing my mind.

We all jumped at the sound of the doorbell. I raced to the door where I was greeted by two officers in uniform. My heart fell into the bottom of my stomach.

"Hello, are the parents of Nathan Davenport here?"

"I'm his mother," I said too quietly. My emotions were getting the best of me.

Tanya stepped next to me and put her hand in mine.

"I'm his stepmother and my husband, his father, is in the hospital how can we help you officer?"

"Please don't tell me my son is dead," I said fearing the worse.

"No ma'am your son isn't dead, but could you come down to the precinct with us. I'm afraid there has been an accident."

"An accident?" I screamed.

Jason rushed to my side for support.

"Is Nathan alright?" Tanya asked.

She sounded just as worried as I did.

The officers looked at each other.

"It would be best if you just came down to the station and we can discuss it further."

Grabbing my purse and keys, I headed out the door followed by Jason and Tanya.

"Give me the keys I'll drive," Jason said.

"Thanks," I replied.

We all hopped in my four-door Honda and drove to the police station. I prayed on the way there that my son wasn't harmed in anyway.

Portia

That ugly white girl had some nerve hitting me in my damn mouth. She just doesn't know who she is fucking with. If it weren't for Jason holding me back I would have put a whooping on that ass something serious. I was almost thinking about moving in that big stupid ass house too.

Before coming to the party an eviction notice was waiting for me on my door. I had to hurry up and snatch it down so the kids wouldn't see. Thankfully Terrance's mama had the kids today because I was in no shape to be with them. I loved my kids, but the closer Terrance got to meet his maker the less I wanted to be around them. I don't know what's going on with me. I am sad they are losing their father I really am. I should be used to death by now. My father was killed in a bad drug deal when I was sixteen. My mother and I have no type of relationship at all. I have no sisters and only one brother whose serving a life sentence for murder.

I need a drink!

I found a bottle of vodka under my kitchen cabinet. Opening it, I poured it down my throat until it didn't burn anymore.

I must have passed out on the couch because when I came to it was ten o' clock at night.

Damn!

I had been sleep for four hours. When I tried to sit up I felt a throbbing pain on the side of my head. The glare from the 52" flat screen TV on the wall had me shielding my eyes. The news reporter, Callie Washington from Channel 6 action news was live reporting a three alarm fire.

That girl needs her damn hair done. I should drive down there and give her my card.

I heard my cell phone ringing as I grabbed a Newport from my purse. I picked up a couple of bad habits over the past few months from all the stress. I lit the square and blew the smoke out before looking at the caller ID.

It was Shavonne. Lord knows I did not want to talk to her or anyone else for that matter. I got up and dragged my feet along the carpet. My cell phone rang again. This time it was Brandy, one of my stylists. She probably wanted to call in as she had been doing all week. She met one of those dope boys on the Southside and thought she hit it big when he bought her a Range Rover. I told that girl she had better stop calling in or he was going to have to buy her more than a damn truck!

I walked down the hall towards my bedroom and caught a glimpse of my body in the mirror on the wall. I had put on a couple of extra pounds. More than likely it was from all the drinking and smoking I had been doing over the past few months. I turned and looked at my ass. It was still nice and round so the extra weight was doing me a bit of good.

Nicki Minaj ain't got shit on me.

I shook my ass a little bit so it would bounce.

As bad as I need money I should take my ass to the strip club and make a little change.

I laughed out loud.

My cell phone rang again. I had it in my hand and was ready to answer it and curse out whoever was on the other end. I noticed it was Tanya calling. I hit the ignore button right away. I had nothing to say to her and she had nothing to say to me. She let that white bitch attack me at the party so I was good on any conversation she had for me.

I set the phone down on the bathroom sink, took my clothes off, and hopped in the shower. The hot water on my skin was so relaxing. I tried to relax, but I heard my house phone ringing in my bedroom.

Whoever had my house number could leave a fucking message. I grabbed my Amber Romance body wash by Victoria's Secret and lathered it up on my skin. I tried to breathe in the aroma so I could relax until I heard someone screaming on my answering machine.

"Portia, pick up the phone. I know your ass is home! I am outside! Come answer the door something bad has happened!"

That was the sound of my friend Keisha's voice. I hopped out the shower, grabbed a towel, and ran to my front door.

Snatching it open I asked,

"Who died?"

She stormed in past me.

"You are about to! Have you been watching the news? Did Brandy or Shavonne get a hold of you?"

"I saw them calling. What's going on that brought your fat ass to my front door?"

She gave me a look for calling her fat and grabbed the remote to my TV. Keisha was a big girl and weighed at least three hundred pounds. We had been friends forever, so she knew I had the tendency to talk shit every now and then.

"You are pitiful you know that," she said.

She turned up the volume until the news was blasting through the surround sound speakers.

"We are live on the scene at a three alarm fire that has traffic at a standstill. Firefighters have been battling the blaze for the last thirty minutes. Witnesses on the scene say they believe it was arson."

"Okay big deal there is a fire on the north side of Chicago. Those happen all the time."

She gave me a look.

"Have you been drinking again? Look at the name on the building."

I looked at the TV and saw the sign I had made for my shop as it was being sprayed with water. My heart skipped a beat and dropped in my stomach when I realized it was my salon that was on fire.

"Why didn't someone call me?"

"We tried to call you! Shavonne and Brandy have been blowing your cell phone up. They called me knowing I was the only one who lived close by and had your house number. They also called......Terrance."

Keisha looked at me for a reaction.

"What the fuck for? That's not his shop! Who in the hell told them to call Terrance?"

"Portia, he is a partner and he gave you the money to open the shop. He is listed on the contact list in the event of an emergency when you can't be reached."

That would explain why Tanya called.

My shop, the center of my being next to my children was burning right before my eyes. I had to get down there and do something. I put on my shoes that were by the door, grabbed my keys, and headed out to my car.

"Where are you going in a towel?"

I ignored her as I ran to my car and unlocked the doors.

Keisha came running to the car before I could even get it started.

"You got to be the craziest bitch I know. Move. I'll drive. Put your clothes on."

She threw a t-shirt and a pair of jogging pants at me. I pulled my towel down and threw on the t-shirt minus a bra and slid the jogging pants over my naked ass. As she pulled off I saw my next door neighbor standing in his driveway looking at me with a nasty smile on his face. I rolled down my window.

"What you looking at old man? This pussy here is not for you!"

Keisha rolled up the window before I could say anything else.

"Have you no shame?" She asked.

I thought about it for a second.

"Nope sure don't."

"I swear if you weren't my friend I would hate you."

I just waved her comment off.

By the time we arrived my shop was nothing more than a steaming pile of mess. Because it was in a strip mall it had caught the other buildings on fire as well. There was yellow caution tape in front of the melted doorway.

"I'm sorry you can't go in there," the firefighter said to me.

"It's my shop! I can go wherever I please."

"Ma'am it's too dangerous. I can't let you in there right now."

I could still smell the scent of burnt wood and feel the warmth in the air the blaze had created.

I didn't feel the tears that were on my face until they hit my hand. I quickly wiped them away.

I noticed Tanya's black BMW parked nearby and I knew she had to be on the scene somewhere.

"Does anyone know where the owner of this car is?"

"I'm right here Portia," she said

Tanya walked over to me with her hand on her stomach.

"Do you have the number for the insurance company so we can make sure any losses are recovered?"

I dropped my head.

"Don't tell me you haven't been paying the premiums!" She yelled.

I looked away.

"Oh my God, Terrance gave you money every month to pay the insurance, Portia!"

Tanya started pacing back and forth. Keisha was nearby and just shook her head at me.

"I needed that money. How else was I supposed to run a shop, take care of his two kids, and pay my bills?"

I wasn't going to tell her some of that money was used to purchase my new Gucci bag, the matching boots, and some new jewelry.

"Are you serious right now? Your ass stays in the mall. Every time I see you, you smell like alcohol and stale cigarettes. You are always rocking designer jeans, shoes, and purses. Maybe if you stop trying to impress Terrance with that bullshit you would have taken care of your business," she said.

I laughed before responding,

"What are you talking about? I don't have to impress anyone who is already impressed with me!"

Keisha shot me a look.

"Portia, you just haven't gotten it through your head that Terrance doesn't want you," Tanya said while putting her hand on her belly. This broad was always touching her damn stomach like she was carrying Jesus.

I wanted to set Tanya straight and let her know how clueless she was about her husband. No one could tell me Terrance didn't want me. It was in his eyes. I see it in the way he looks at me whenever I seen him.

"Look boo, I know you think your husband is all that, but what good is he to me now? Dead dick can't do shit for me!"

That was the best thing I could say to her without revealing my true feelings.

"Portia! Do you have to be so insensitive?" Keisha said.

"Poor hood rat doesn't know any better." Tanya stood there shaking her head.

"Who in the hell are you calling a hood rat you uppity ass bitch?"

I was getting tired of Tanya and Amber acting like they had balls dangling between their thighs. The nerve of either one trying to step to me and actually start something without me finishing it was just crazy.

Keisha grabbed my arm before I could react.

"I could slap the mess out of you again right now for disrespecting my husband like that, but instead what I'm going to do is pray for you. That's how sorry I feel for you," Tanya said.

"I don't need your prayers or your sorry feelings. You better get out of my face." I stepped closer to Tanya ready to knock her pregnant ass right on the concrete.

Keisha stood in front of me.

"Why are you in my way?" I asked her.

This chic was supposed to be on my side.

"You don't need to stop her. If she is going to do something let her do it," Tanya said.

"Ya'll are tripping right now. How long are you two going to keep fighting?" Keisha asked.

Before I could respond a police officer approached us.

"Is everything alright over here ladies?" He asked.

"Yes officer, everything is fine. I was just getting ready to leave. I will deal with you later," Tanya replied. She threw me a look before walking off towards her car and skirting off.

I just rolled my eyes.

"I can't stand her uppity ass," I said.

"That is probably because you are jealous of her," Keisha said.

Is she on drugs?

"Think about it. She has the house, the man, the cars, and she will get most of the money when he dies."

A thought came to my mind that stopped me from cursing her out.

"She won't get anything if I have something to do with it."

"I don't even want to know what you plan to do."

"Don't worry about it I won't be telling you anyway."

No money to cover the damages to my shop, no money to pay my rent, or feed my kids.

I had to put a plan into action and fast. I just hoped it worked.

Tanya

I wish I could just leave Chicago. All this drama that keeps on happening is just too much. First, Nathan disappears, and then the police drag us down to the station saying he is guilty of arson, but they have no evidence that he did so they had to let him go. The same night Portia's salon catches fire and I found out her dumb ass didn't pay the insurance premium.

I had to pause in my thoughts.

Could Nathan have started the fire at Portia's shop?

I immediately dismissed the thought. Nathan was a good kid he would never do a thing like that.

Sitting at the airport, I watched as Jason's plane lifted in to the air on its way back to Atlanta. He had to get back for an important meeting.

He stayed the night with me before he left and just held me all night long while stroking my hair and rubbing my belly, all the things Terrance used to do before the cancer overtook him. I just wish having him around didn't feel so good. My visits to Terrance at the hospital became less and less. I just couldn't face him. He no longer resembled the man I fell in love with. That strong handsome man everyone wanted. Now he was just weak and frail on the verge of dying.

What the hell am I saying?

I was supposed to be there for my husband "*until death does us part.*" Trying to handle everything by myself was wreaking havoc on my body. I was barely eating and I had no one to talk to. I wish I had some real female friends that I could vent my frustrations to.

I decided to call my sister Janine.

"Hey J, it's me Tanya."

"Hey little sis, how are you holding up?" She asked.

I knew she was only showing concern, but that question pissed me off.

"I wish everyone would stop asking me that. I am not holding up that's just it. I'm tired! I'm sick of sitting here waiting on Terrance to die. It's so frustrating. I know I'm his wife and I'm supposed to be supportive, but I am getting tired!"

The tears came out of nowhere followed by the sharp pain in my abdomen.

"I can imagine how you feel. Are you okay? You are breathing funny," Janine said.

I tried to answer her but the pain I felt was followed by another pain. I doubled over trying to hold on to the end table.

"Janine something is wrong. I'm having sharp stomach pains."

I was on my knees in tears.

"I'm going to call 911 just hang in there. I'll be there as fast as I can."

I dropped the phone and fell to the floor. I felt a very sharp pain followed by something warm and wet between my legs. I didn't want to face the horror of what I knew might be happening. When I touched in between my legs and looked at my hands they were red. I was having a miscarriage. I balled up into a fetal position as more painful cramps followed.

Once the ambulance arrived my sister came running through the door.

"Oh my God, Tanya!" She screamed.

I knew it had to be bad from the look on her face and the pain I was feeling. The paramedics put me on a gurney and wheeled me out into the ambulance.

Inside my sister sat holding my hand while someone checked my vitals. The thought of not being pregnant both sickened and elated me at the same time. I know that has to sound bad, but why would I bring a child into this world knowing I will have to raise it alone? I didn't feel like explaining how Terrance used to be to a new child that would never know him.

We arrived at Mercy West hospital, the same hospital they were keeping Terrance at. Watching the lights on the ceiling as they rushed me into an operating room made me dizzy. I felt a hand on my arm as I was being whisked away and thought I seen Jesus.

This can't be my time to die!

The light was getting brighter and brighter until everything went dark.

Amber

Sitting in my accounting class I couldn't focus. Nathan was almost charged with arson the night of Terrance's party. He claims he left to get away from all the drama at the house. Police tried to place him at the scene of a fire at a hair shop that happened to be owned by Terrance and Portia. Since there was no concrete evidence that he was there, they had to let him go. I begged one of the officers, who knew my mother not to call her, but he did anyway. She hasn't let me hear the end of going to Terrance's party and being around *"those people."*

You still love Terrance!

Those words Rebecca said kept ringing back in my head and the way he held onto my hand at the party. There was no way I still loved him.

We hadn't been together in over thirteen years. He had three more kids in between that time and had gotten married.

When I fall in love, I fall hard. Long, deep, and hard. Just the way I like my men. What I can't seem to understand is why I am usually falling by myself.

I think I am very attractive. I'm not your typical white girl with the blond hair, blue eyed, big breasts, and flat ass image. I have chestnut brown hair and my eyes are brown. My butt sort of sprouted out of nowhere after I gave birth to Nathan. It's not huge but it's there. My size 36D breasts always turn heads when I wear certain shirts.

I am still not sure why Terrance and I split in the first place. I know it was because of my mother, but he still should never have left me pregnant and alone. He should have fought for me. I believe that is what holds me back from being able to get into a decent relationship. After all these years I still don't have any real closure.

122

"Ms. Sykowski can you explain problem fourteen for the class?'

I snapped back to reality and realized the professor was calling my name.

"Um...I... well...."

I stumbled over my words feeling like a damn fool. I fumbled with my papers and they fell to the floor. I felt a hand on mine helping me pick them up. When I looked up I was looking into the face of a very handsome black man.

"Thank you."

He smiled.

"No problem sweetheart. The name is Tony."

He reached out his hand. I look around to see if anyone was looking. I like black men, but a lot of black women automatically turn their nose up at me when they see one of them trying to talk to me. When I noticed everyone's attention was back on the professor, I shook the man's hand.

"Nice meeting you Tony. Is that short for something?"

He laughed.

"Why does everyone ask that? You don't think I could just be named Tony without being Antonio or Anthony? "

I couldn't help but smile.

"I guess you could."

"You want to grab a coffee after class?"

Did he just ask me for a date? No wait he said coffee.

I was getting too anxious already.

"Sure coffee sounds warm."

He laughed again.

"I'm sorry that was corny right?"

"No, coffee is warm, but you didn't say you wanted to get some with me. It's because I'm black isn't it?"

"What! No! Are you black I didn't even notice?"

He laughed again.

"You are funny......," he stopped midsentence, waiting for my name.

"My name is Amber....Amber Sy..Sykowski."

Please don't let this man know my mother or my family.

"Amber, huh, like the color of your eyes. It's nice to meet you."

I giggled feeling like a school girl. He turned back around and I couldn't wait for class to be over.

Tony was a gentleman, opening the door, and pulling out my chair once we were inside the school café. We sat down over mocha latte's talking about Professor Wiggin's class. I found myself attracted to him in a way. His teeth were white, his hair was low cut, but he was a bit on the short and chunky side. I say he had to be about five-six because I stand about five-five and when I look at him we are practically eye to eye. His personality made up for what he lacked height wise. The more he talked the more I liked what he had to say.

Lord knows I haven't had a man in years. My body was getting real tired of being vibrated to death when I needed a quick fix, and dildos just weren't the same as being wrapped up in someone's arms. I needed to feel a real man holding me, and calling out my name.

"Amber?"

I looked at him with a guilty expression unaware that he had been calling my name while I was thinking about sex.

"Are you okay?" He asked.

"Yea I'm okay. It's just been a long day."

"I'm sorry. I'm probably talking too much," he said.

"No, you are fine really."

"Are you sure?"

"I'm sorry I have just been going through a lot lately."

He touched my hand and smiled. I squeezed my legs together feeling like a horny teenager.

"Well, whatever it is if you ever want to talk about it I am here for you. You really are a beautiful woman. I'd love to be able to take you out to dinner sometime if you let me."

"Sure I'd let you. I mean that would be nice."

I could have kicked myself for sounding so desperate.

"So how does tomorrow night around 7 o' clock sound?"

"Sounds good."

"Great! I can pick you up, or if you want to meet me here at the café that would be fine too."

I thought about my mother and what she would say seeing him on our doorstep. It was definitely time for me to move out.

"I can meet you here at the café."

I gave him my phone number and got up to attend my next class. I was happier than I had ever been finally going out on a real date. I also decided if I moved in the house Terrance had purchased it might be easier for me to date without any issues. I needed to make some phone calls.

Portia

Sitting outside the front of the house Terrance bought in Highland Park, I contemplated my decision. I could blast Tanya's infidelity to Terrance's attorney and she wouldn't get a dime of Terrance's money. At least I think. I know on some of those courts TV shows if the woman cheated the man owed her nothing since she broke the vows. I could move in with my kids and be set for life with her out of the way. I could make sure that white bitch Amber didn't step foot near the house either.

What did I have to lose?

I had two of Terrance's kids while they only had one. That put me in the front seat of needing more money than they would. I pulled out my blackberry that was buzzing away in my pocket.

"What?" I screamed

"Is that how you answer the phone?"

I rolled my eyes. It was Terrance's sister, Tina.

"Hey Tina, my apologies it's a lot going on."

"I know. I just called to let you know Teyah and TJ aren't at daycare. I was wondering if you had picked them up," she asked.

"What do you mean they aren't at daycare? I dropped them off this morning."

At least I think I did.

"I went to go get them as I normally do and the daycare lady said they aren't there."

"Well, where in the hell could they be?" I screamed at her.

"Stop de yelling, mon. I told you what I know and dat is all. I will make some phone calls to see if my ma or dad picked them up. I will call you back."

She disconnected the call on me.

If I had married her brother, she and her entire family would be deported back to Jamaica, although, I wasn't sure if she was an American citizen already.

Everyone is starting to get on my nerves.

I reached in my purse and pulled out two mini bottles of Grey Goose I had bought from the store. The warmth from the alcohol warmed me up against the chilly Chicago wind. I got out the car, pulled my Baby Phat pea-coat tighter around my body, and walked up the driveway towards the house. I looked inside the front window and noticed a figure in the shadows moving around.

Inside the person was moving boxes and setting things up on the table. I ran to the front door and rang the doorbell repeatedly thinking it was Tanya or Amber.

I'd be damned if these bitches beat me to moving in this house first.

Some Mexican looking chic answered the door.

"May I help you?" She asked.

"What are you doing here?"

"I'm sorry who are you?" She frowned at me.

"Don't worry about who I am why you are in my house?"

She looked around and then laughed.

"I don't know what you were told, but this house belongs to me."

I looked at her like she was crazy.

"How does this house belong to you?"

She smiled and opened the door.

"Do come in. Would you like something to drink?"

I was going to decline coming in until she offered something to drink.

"What do you have?" I said while stepping inside.

The foyer had marble flooring and was partially decorated with a cherry wood table and a matching mirror. I followed her through the massive dining room and into the kitchen. She pulled out a glass from one of the cabinets.

"All I have is some Merlot," she said.

"That's fine."

She handed me the glass. I took a sip of the warm liquid and looked around. The cabinets were mahogany in color and the stainless steel fridge and stove top range set it off perfectly. I was definitely impressed. I didn't get to see this part of the house at the party.

"My name is Mariah Gonzalez."

She put out her hand for me to shake it. I reluctantly put my hand in hers and gave a firm shake.

"We are selling this house to a man by the name of Terrance Davenport. Do you know him?"

"Yes I do."

"So you're Tanya?" She asked.

"Hell no, I'm Portia. Unfortunately, Tanya is his wife."

Mariah paused. There was an awkward silence before she continued.

"Oh I see. Well I came by to set up some furniture pieces to convince Terrance to buy the house by adding some flair to it."

I took the last sip of wine from the glass before setting it on the counter. The glass clinked against the marble a bit too loud and I realized I was a bit tipsy.

"So, he hasn't bought it yet?" I asked.

"No. He said he was waiting on some type of *"arrangement"* he set up to go through before he made an offer." Mariah replied.

There goes that damn arrangement being brought up again.

"How many bedrooms does this place have?"

"There are seven bedrooms. Would you like a tour?" She asked me.

"Sure, why not."

She took me around to each bedroom that had its own bathroom with a separate Jacuzzi tub in each room, along with a giant walk-in closet. This house made my condo look like a damn broom closet. There was a computer room and a study with built in book shelves. The basement looked like a mini gym used to be there from the mirrors on the wall, and the treadmill in the corner. If I chose to move in first I could have whatever room I wanted and say so on everything.

Yes, that is what I would do. I would move in!

"I am sold."

Mariah laughed.

"I'm glad you are, but unless you have the money to go ahead with the sale I need you to let Terrance know that you like it."

"That's not a problem I was on my way to the hospital to see him now," I paused at one of the floor to ceiling windows.

"Hospital, is everything alright?" Mariah asked alarmed.

I frowned. *How could she not know Terrance was dying?*

"Yeah, that's where Terrance is," I said nonchalantly.

"Oh I didn't realize that. Is he a doing a job there?"

She couldn't be serious. She really had no clue about his wellbeing or lack thereof. I wasn't going to tell her in case it messed up any chances of him purchasing the house.

"No, he isn't working. Listen, I need to go. I have to get my kids from daycare before it gets late," I headed towards the spiral staircase in the middle of the hallway.

"Okay well Terrance has my number and if he is going to make an offer he needs to do so soon. We have held off on the sale long enough."Mariah replied.

I thanked Mariah for the tour, got back in my car, and drove to Mercy hospital. I went straight up to Terrance's room and noticed his room was empty. Walking back into the hallway I approached the nurse's station.

"Excuse me nurse where is the patient that was in this room?" I pointed at Terrance's door.

She looked at me before looking at her chart.

"Are you referring to Mr. Davenport?"

I nodded my head.

"He was discharged this morning," she said then turned her back and continued on about her job like I wasn't still standing there.

What the hell?

"What do you mean discharged? How do you send a cancer patient on his death bed, home?" I all but screamed at her.

I thought I saw this heffa roll her eyes at me. *Who does she think she is?*

"Are you a relative? If not, then I am not allowed to release that information to you."

"You damn right I'm a relative now tell me where Terrance is!"

The nurse sighed loudly.

"He said he no longer wanted to be at the hospital, so he was discharged to his care team of nurses and sent home. We have actually been trying to reach Mr. Davenport to let him know his *wife* came in this morning by ambulance," she said. When she mentioned the word wife she gave me a look. I ignored it and probed her further.

"Tanya was here? What for?" I asked.

"You sure have a lot of questions. Are you related to Mrs. Davenport?"

"Yes something like that."

Another nurse walked up on the tail end of our conversation.

"Oh good, is this someone here for Mrs. Davenport?" I saw the nurse I was talking to give me a look while I nodded my head. The other nurse continued without pause. "She is in the recovery unit right now. Her appendix burst so she had to have emergency surgery this morning. Unfortunately, the doctors were unable to save the baby."

So Tanya lost her baby.Hmph! I wanted to feel sorry for her, but I couldn't. That just kept me in the running for having his two kids. *Score.* Tanya zero. Amber one. *Ha bitches!*

"Did you want her room number?"

I gave the nurse a look.

"Uh no…. I'll come back to visit umm…later thanks."

I had to leave and go talk to Terrance right away so I could get dibs on the crib before my shit was sitting out on the curbside tomorrow morning.

Terrance

Hanging on to what little bit of life I could was a real fucking struggle. My days were numbered. All I wanted to know was why did I have to die now?

Amber, Tanya and Portia were all being hardheaded. None of them would move into the new house. I heard about Portia's shop burning down. If I had even a small amount of strength I would have beat her ass for not paying the insurance premiums. Investing in her dream was a big mistake. I wanted my kids to be okay, so I felt by getting their momma off her ass and putting her in a situation that would benefit her, it would be fruitful.

Once again she was going to need me and soon. I had her evicted out of her condo and was getting ready to have her Mustang repossessed until she crashed it. I felt bad for having to go about things this way, but as they say *"a hardhead makes a soft ass"*.

My mother told me to never hit a woman so I had to hit them all where it hurt the most, their livelihood and wellbeing. Since they all decided not to listen to my final wishes, I would make their lives hell and they would all come groveling, Tanya included.

I knew my wife had some type of thing for Jason in the way that she looked at him. She used to look at me the same way. With her being pregnant and me being sick, I couldn't satisfy her like I used to so it didn't surprise me that she would look at my best friend with lust. When I emailed him about it he confirmed my suspicions. I couldn't get mad because hell he was the next best thing. I didn't want any random nigga touching my wife.

I gave him the go ahead to do what I knew he had earned a reputation for back in college, eating pussy! People may think I'm sick for that, but I take care of mine in every way possible.

The agreement was for him not to stick his dick in her until I was dead. That was something I just couldn't deal with no matter how sick I was. Besides, she was carrying my child.

Instead of Tanya coming to me about the situation that I knew occurred she chose to hide.

What type of shit is that?

"Mr. Davenport, there is a Portia here to see you," the nurse said interrupting my thoughts.

"You can let her in," I directed.

She must have received the sheriff's notice on her door.

Portia walked in dressed in some tight ass jeans that made her big ass look even bigger. *I doubt if that girl owns anything that actually fits properly.* The shirt she was wearing made her breasts look like two midgets climbed inside and bent over on her chest.

Damn I hate being sick!

I missed putting her legs on my shoulders and banging her back out, and Portia allowed me to do whatever I wanted to her body.

"Well don't you look like a dying mess! Just because you are, doesn't mean you have to look like it Terrance, damn!"

She sat her big purse down in the chair.

"Why are you here?" I asked her.

"I came to tell you I'll move in the stupid house and do this arrangement bullshit!"

I sat up in the bed as much as I could without pain.

"Really, what made you change your mind?" I was curious to know.

"I want to fulfill whatever wish you ask of me."

I laughed out loud.

This bitch was lying. Portia didn't give a damn about me, or anyone else for that matter. All she wanted was the luxuries in life.

"You are a real head case you know that, but I'm glad you changed your mind," I told her.

"Yea and I met Mariah Gonzales at the house. She said you need to call her and make an offer."

That surprised me.

"Why was Mariah at the house?" I said more to myself than to Portia but she answered me anyway.

"Hell if I know. She said she wanted to convince you to buy it, or they are going to sell it to someone else."

I looked at her. I could tell Portia was tipsy and she smelled like alcohol. That concerned me that she was starting to turn into a real drunk. I looked over at the clock near the bedside. It was only 2 o'clock.

"Portia, damn it's not even happy hour and you already been drinking." I watched a guilty expression cross her face.

"Why is everyone so concerned about what the fuck I do with my life? If I want to drink for breakfast, lunch, and dinner that's my damn business."

The nurse interrupted us before I could scold her again.

"Mr. Davenport I'm sorry to interrupt you again, but there are two police officers at the door that need to ask you some questions."

I looked at Portia who looked at me curiously.

"It's ok you can send them in," I instructed.

"You and I are not done yet," I pointed to Portia. She rolled her eyes.

A male officer entered the room accompanied by a female officer.

"Mr. and Mrs. Davenport?" He asked.

"I'm Mr. Davenport, Mrs. Davenport is not here."

Portia rolled her eyes again.

"Are you the father of Terrance and Teyah Davenport?"

"Yes I am officer is there a problem?"

I looked over at Portia again. I knew in my gut she had something to do with this.

"I am their mother. What's wrong with my kids?" She asked.

The officers looked at one another before looking back at Portia.

"You're the mother?" The female officer asked.

Portia abruptly stood up. I noticed both officers put their hands near their weapons.

"Yes I am their mama what the hell is going on? Did TJ steal something again? I told that boy to stop doing that shit."

"Ma'am, please you might want to sit down!" The officer instructed.

"Why do I need to sit down? Where are my kids?" Portia remained standing.

"Excuse me officer please tell me what's going on!" I was getting anxious waiting on them to get to the point. The male officer pulled out his pad and read from it,

"Mr. Davenport, someone found your children wandering alone this morning around six a.m. The little boy was holding the hand of a very small girl about two years old. He told witnesses he was walking her to daycare since their mother never came home. The little girl got too close to a river embankment and fell in the water. Your son jumped in to save her. Someone passing by saw them when they fell and tried to rescue them."

Portia screamed,

"Where are they, are they okay?"

The officers dropped their heads and I knew what they were about to say.

"I'm sorry by the time the ambulance arrived the little girl couldn't be resuscitated. Your son is in critical condition suffering from major head trauma, and water in his lungs," the officer concluded.

Portia screamed again and collapsed to the floor.

"Ma'am we are going to have to place you under arrest," the female officer said.

I couldn't speak. I struggled to maintain my composure to get an understanding of what was happening.

"Why is she being arrested?" I asked.

"She is going to be arrested for child neglect and child endangerment. A neighbor saw her this morning stumbling drunk. They said she must have slept it off in her car before pulling off without the children."

I was angry, sad, and shocked all at the same time. The familiar pains in my chest begin to creep up. I watched as the officers struggled to pull a grief stricken Portia from the floor to handcuff her.

"I'm sorry. I'm so sorry, Terrance you have to believe me!" She cried out.

I couldn't feel sorry for her. I was sorry I let my children suffer at her hands without intervening. I was supposed to die first not my child. The pain hurt worse than the cancer that was spreading throughout my body. I had to call Tanya and let her know.

The tears began falling faster from my eyes and the pain of losing my daughter tore through my soul. I felt responsible for her death. If I had not of evicted Portia from her condo maybe she would not have taken to drinking as much. The problems I was placing on her for my own selfish gain had taken its toll on everyone. I was tired of causing pain. I had caused damage to the women in my life and two of my children suffered because of it.

Please Lord forgive me for what I have done!

I collapsed back on the bed and wept for the life of my only daughter.

Tanya

I felt empty and broken. The doctors actually made me deliver my dead fetus, because I was too far along for them to do the D & C procedure of sucking it out. I was horrified having to push out my dead son. Everything was crumbling around me. I missed my husband terribly.

And Jason!

My sister stayed by my side throughout the entire ordeal. I knew it was time to face the music and tell Terrance about my affair with Jason if you can even call it that. My sister begged me not to telling me, "eating aint cheating" and that me telling him could kill him. Maybe she is right, but I think anything whether it's kissing, touching, fondling, or mouth to genital contact with someone you are not married to can be considered cheating. I was lost.

When I called up to his room they told me they had released him to home care since he refused to stay at the hospital any longer. This was going to be harder than I initially thought. The doctors kept me in the hospital for observation for a week before they sent me home.

Upon entering my home the atmosphere seemed different, cold even. I heard sobs coming from the room. The nurse appeared from the kitchen.

"Hey Tanya, how are you feeling?" She gave me a gentle hug.

"I'm still in a bit of pain, but I have some good meds, and I'm doing better than I was," I responded. She looked down at my stomach wanting to ask about the baby but I could tell she was afraid to.

"It's okay I'm dealing with it. It's weird not feeling him in there anymore."

I instinctively put my hand on my stomach before I realized what I had done. I still looked pregnant, but I definitely didn't feel it.

The nurse touched my hand with tears in her eyes. We were silent for a few seconds. I could still hear the sobs in the distance.

"Is that Terrance?" I asked her.

"Yes, I'm afraid something terrible has happened. He has been crying all day. I think he may be trying to kill himself. He hasn't eaten, won't take his meds, and he isn't sleeping much at all. The other nurse will be here to relieve me shortly. He won't let me in the room, so I have to keep checking his vitals from the monitor in the living room. I hope you don't mind."

I looked around the living room at all of the medical equipment that was sitting in it. It had been transformed into a makeshift hospital triage.

"No that's okay. You can go now if you'd like. I'll tell the other nurse when she gets here."

The nurse looked at me.

"Are you sure? He is in pretty bad shape. I know you aren't physically up to dealing with it."

I was used to being alone with him and dealing with his sickness, so I knew this time would be no different.

"It's nothing I haven't handled before," I told her.

"Oh, but it's not the cancer that has him in so much pain."

I looked at the nurse confused. She continued,

"Portia was by here earlier and the police came and arrested her. I don't know the full story on why, but ever since then he's been crying nonstop."

I know this man was not crying over his baby momma going to jail. I was going to make him cry even harder if that was the reason. I set my purse down and went to the den where they had put his hospital bed. I lightly tapped the door before gently pushing it open.

"Go away," Terrance yelled.

"Terrance, it's me Tanya."

He was quiet. I pushed the door open so that I could enter the room and found him covering his eyes.

"Honey, what's the matter?" I asked.

I looked at my husband. His face was pale and he looked thinner than he had before. Patches of his hair had grown back and his lips were cracked dry.

"She's gone! She's gone! Tanya she is gone!"

I knew he couldn't be referring to Portia. There was just no way.

"Who's gone?" I had to know.

"Teyah, she's gone and it's my fault."

"Teyah? What? Where did she go?"

He looked at me with a pained expression.

"My baby is dead. She's dead. I killed her," Terrance started sobbing again.

I was confused. I wasn't sure if I comprehended correctly.

"What happened to Teyah?" I asked.

Terrance gave me that painful expression again.

"Tanya she's dead! She fell over in some water and drowned," he continued to sob.

"What do you mean she's dead? Where was her mother when this happened? What about TJ? Where is TJ?"

I surprised myself by how defensive my tone had become.

Terrance just shook his head and continued to cry. He stopped for a second catching his breath and then he spoke,

"Portia was drunk and ended up leaving the kids at home this morning. The neighbors said TJ tried to walk Teyah to daycare and you know that river embankment she lives by?" I nodded my head. " TJ's foot slipped and they fell in the..."

He couldn't finish his sentence. He was overcome with grief. I moved closer, sitting down on his bed. The tears started pouring from my eyes.

I held Terrance in my arms as our tears mixed together. I cried for my son, and Teyah, although she wasn't my natural child. I wanted to hurt Portia for causing all this pain to my family.

After a while, we both stopped crying. Terrance's eyes were puffy and red around the rim.

"Baby, is TJ okay?" I asked softly while rubbing his head.

Terrance shook his head.

"He is in intensive care."

There was a moment of silence as I could tell he was thinking about it. He turned his attention back to me and stared at me. I suddenly felt self-conscious. I felt his hand rub my stomach that was now softer since there was no baby inside of it.

"My son, where is he?" He asked.

The words were stuck in my throat. He was already facing enough trauma why would I add to it.

"Tanya, answer me where is my son?"

Fresh tears started to spill down my cheeks.

"Tanya!"

"I lost him Terrance! He's dead too!"

Sobs shook my body as the pain of losing my baby overwhelmed me. Terrance encircled his arms around me and kissed the top of my hair.

"I'm so sorry baby. I'm sorry I wasn't there for you."

He held on to me with all the strength he had left and we sat crying for our babies. After almost two hours I was finally able to coax him into eating and taking his pain meds. The nurse came by and took over while I went to lie down in our bedroom. The bed was still just the way I had left it. I pulled back the burgundy satin comforter and turned down a corner of my sheets. I climbed in the King size bed and felt an instant chill. My bed was cold and empty.

It was the way I felt my life was starting to be. I tried to close my eyes, but my thoughts turned to Jason.

I couldn't get him out of my mind. I don't know if it was the oral sex, or the fact that I had unresolved issues with my husband and his kids' mother's.

I think I was using Jason as an outlet for the pain I was experiencing. I had to call him so I could hear his voice.

He answered on the first ring.

"Hello?"

"Hey Jason."

There was silence on his end.

"Uh.. hey… who is this?"

"It's Tanya."

"Tanya…Tanya who?"

"Tanya Davenport."

I heard him shuffling around in the background like he was moving before he responded.

"Hey Tanya what's wrong? Is everything okay? Is Terrance…?"

"No Jason he's not dead. I just called because…… I miss you."

There was an awkward silence on his end again and I felt stupid for calling.

"Okay well listen T, I have to go, but I'll call you back later."

The call disconnected.

I wasn't sure how to take that. Maybe he had company. I didn't give that a thought. He wasn't my man, so I couldn't get jealous. I just didn't like how he rushed me off the phone and acted so nonchalant. I needed to let go of whatever thought I had of him and focus on the matter at hand.

My husband!

I looked around the room for the bottle of morphine pills the doctor had prescribed me. I wasn't in any real pain, but I needed something to soothe the pain I was feeling in my heart. I popped two pills and pulled the covers up over my head as the tears ran down my face.

Portia

Sitting in a jail cell with a bunch of musty ass women and one toilet is something I would never wish on my worst enemy. Well, maybe one or two of them, but this was some bullshit! I couldn't believe those damn cops arrested me. What hurts the most is my baby is dead and I won't be able to see her sweet innocent face anymore. I felt responsible, but at the same time I didn't. It wasn't my fault. Life dealt me a bad hand and I had to drink the pain away. I just didn't realize how much I was really drinking. My habit started when I was younger. Every time I met up with Terrance we drank. It was just what you did as a teenager to make whatever you were doing that much better. Being tipsy was how I got through most of my days.

"Aye Ma."

I turned around to see this manly look woman with facial hair trying to get my attention.

"What's a pretty thing like you up in a joint like this for?"

I turned up my nose at her.

"I tried to kill a woman!"

She gave me a look before smiling.

"Damn, you too, how did you do it? I stabbed my old lady in the chest several times, but that bitch wouldn't die."

My mouth dropped opened and I got up and moved across the room.

I knew that this was the wrong time to be turning to God, but I needed deliverance fast. Hell, I didn't even know how to pray, or what to pray for.

God please if you can hear me help!

"Excuse me?"

I was talking to the correctional officer standing closest to the holding cell.

"May I please make a phone call?"

He turned around and looked at me.

"What's your name?"

"It's Portia Jackson."

He looked on his sheet.

"Okay Ms. Jackson you get one phone call make it quick."

He came over and unlocked the cell while pointing to the phone sitting on the desk.

I made sure to switch my hips a little bit harder as I walked by thinking maybe I could convince him to let me out. He ignored me.

"Dial nine to get an outside line."

I wasn't sure who to call to get me out of this situation. It was a Friday so I knew they were going to try and keep me held up all weekend.

I had to think. There was no way Terrance would bail me out. *Damn, who could I call?*

I pressed nine and dialed the only number I could think of by heart.

"Hello, this is Cheryl speaking."

"Hey…..Cheryl, this is Portia. Something bad has happened!"

"Portia? Oh my dear lord, what do you mean something bad has happened? Where are you? Why are you calling me from the county number?"

"You know the baby I sent you a picture of a couple of months ago?"

"Yes, my beautiful grandbaby."

"She's dead."

"What? Dead? Oh my Lord Jesus Christ!"

Tears began to well up in my eyes.

"I'm in jail mom! They are going to charge me with child neglect and child endangerment."

"Portia, what have you done?" My mother asked.

"I didn't do anything! She wondered off with TJ and they fell over in an embankment."

"You were drinking weren't you? Just like that no good father of yours, rest his soul. I always knew your ways were going to catch up to you. I tried to warn you. What about TJ is he …dead too?"

I shook my head as the tears began to fall all over again.

"I didn't mean for my babies to get hurt."

"How is their father?" She asked.

"He is laid up in a hospital bed at his house waiting on his maker to greet him."

"Portia, how can you speak of your children's father in such a way?"

"You don't know what I been through."

"Oh my dear I do, Keisha calls and lets me know how you and the kids are doing."

There was a long silence.

"So they say I need $50,000 are you going to help me?" I asked her matter of factly.

"No! I told you before until you do right by me everything you do will fail. Everything! You are on your own baby girl. What hospital is my grandson in? I will make sure that you will never be able to hurt him again."

"Why are you being so mean?"

At this point the tears were streaming down my face.

"You need to sit down and take a good look at yourself and how you have treated people. You can't expect me to run and help you when you don't call, and you don't allow me to see my grandchildren. I will not subject myself to your misery and pain. I am going to get my grandson from that hospital and fight you tooth and nail for custody."

"Oh yea, well you'll lose, Cheryl!"

My mother was quiet.

"Goodbye Portia."

The line went dead. I was fucked. I don't know why I even called her in the first place. We never got along and she was never any use to me anyhow.

"Guard, I need one more call."

He gave me a look.

"Please, I just need to make one more call."

"No need Jackson, you been bailed out."

I look around to see if he was joking.

"I have? Who bailed me out?"

"Me!"

I looked up and saw Keisha standing by the table.

I ran to her and hugged her.

"Oh my goodness friend, thank you."

She pushed me back. When I looked in her eyes there were tears forming.

"I had to put up all of my school money, and most of my savings to get you out. You are going to pay me back. I called your attorney for you and he is working out the details of your case. You owe me big time!"

"Anything, name it!" I was desperate to get out of this place.

"You go to these AA meetings and get sober and you move into the house Terrance purchased along with Amber and Tanya!"

"What are my other options?" I asked.

I looked at her to see if she was serious. The look she was giving me meant she was.

"You have the option to march your ass right back in that jail cell and wait for someone else who cares about you to come get you out!"

I thought about it. Keisha was probably the only one who gave a damn about me even despite the way I treated her.

"Fine, I agree," I said.

"Oh no, it's not that easy sign this."

She handed me a pen and a document detailing what she had just told me. I couldn't believe I was going to agree to this mess. I looked back towards the jail cell at the butch chic that tried to step to me earlier. She smiled and licked her lips. I quickly signed the agreement and watched as she had an officer notarize it. *This bitch was serious. I was really going to have to do this shit.*

We walked out the precinct after I gathered all my belongings together. While walking to her car Keisha turned to me and said,

"You know we have to plan Teyah's funeral."

She looked at me for a response.

"I know I'm just not ready."

"I know but it has to be done. I spoke with Tanya she said Terrance will cover the expenses. You only have to go to the funeral home and pick out a casket."

My heart skipped a beat. Never in a million years did I think I would have to pick out a casket for my child. This shit sucked. I wiped the tears that were sliding down my face. I got in the car and gazed up towards the sun that happened to be shining that day. Keisha was talking to me, but I wasn't listening.

"Did you hear what I said?" She asked me. "I said we found out who burned down the shop!"

I looked at her waiting on her to tell me.

"It was Delilah Fowler."

"Are you fucking kidding me? That bitch burnt my shop down? Where does she live at? Take me there now! She thinks she got a beat down before I will put her six feet....." I stopped because Keisha was giving me a look.

Turning a new leaf was going to be hard for me. No alcohol and moving to a house that I would share with two other women I couldn't stand was a big punishment. I just hope I would make it.

Amber

After deciding to finally move into the house, I had received the news about Terrance's daughter. I feel horrible for all the pain he and Tanya have to deal with. One could only hope that Portia would now change her ways. Terrance on the other hand seems to be holding up despite everything that is going on.

Earlier I had to meet with Rebecca to sign a legal agreement to move into the house. I thought that was a bit farfetched, but I knew he was serious. The hard part for me was telling my mom I was moving out. You would think she would be happy for me considering I was grown, but my mother has always had a hard time letting go. When I think about it I believe my mother just wants control. When I told her we were moving she practically had a heart attack.

"You are moving? Just where do you think you are going to move to with my grandson here in Chicago?" She asked slamming the dishes down in the sink.

I took a breath before speaking.

"It's a house in Lincoln Park."

"Lincoln Park? You don't have enough money for a house in Lincoln Park! I don't even have money for a house in Lincoln Park and I have money! What man are you moving in with?"

"Mom, I am grown! I don't have to give you details on my life. I am moving out of your house and when I get there I will let you know!"

"You listen here young lady, I don't give a damn how grown you are you still have to respect me."

"Mom, how can I give you respect when you don't show me respect. You have been treating me like a child ever since I had Nathan. I have tried to prove to you that I am a good mother and I am capable of being on my own. I appreciate you letting me move back home so I can finish school and save up money, but I am thirty years old. It's time for me to make a life for my son and for myself."

I stared into her eyes waiting for a response.

"Don't run back to me when that asshole throws you and your child out on your ass!"

She stormed away from me. All I could do was shake my head. I wanted her to wish me well but that was a far reach from normal. I continued packing Nathan's stuff and put it into totes. As I was packing Tony was texting me on my cell phone.

Hey gorgeous I want to see you ASAP. ☺

The butterflies in my stomach began to flutter. We had been talking every day since the day we had coffee in the café. He was almost too good to be true. He had no children, owned his own house, and wanted to open his own architect firm. He was in school to finish his degree in architecture and already had some promising leads on employment once he finished the program.

I texted him back,

I'm packing. ☺

He responded,

Let me come help you.

My mother came to mind and I knew I couldn't bring him to her house, but I didn't really care. I text him back the address to my parents house and couldn't wait to see the look on my mother's face when she answered the door and saw that Tony was black.

While I was putting Nathan's shoes in a box I heard my mother scream. I ran downstairs to see what the commotion was about. Tony was standing in the doorway with a shocked expression on his face and my mother had her hand over her mouth. I had never seen her look like that. Nothing ever scared her, but whatever Tony said, or did, had.

"How dare you come to this house?" She screamed at him.

Tony gave me a funny look.

"Mom, what are you talking about?" I asked.

She ignored me.

"You have some nerve showing your face at my home," my mom said to Tony.

"I'm sorry I don't know what you are talking about ma'am. I am here to see Amber."

My mother turned around and her face was white as a ghost.

"Now you want to try and get my daughter?"

I wasn't sure what pipe my mother was smoking but she was acting real strange.

"Can you please excuse us Tony? I am not sure what's going on with my mother."

He nodded his head while I tried to pull my mother into the kitchen.

"I will not let this rapist in my house!"

She yanked her arm away from me and went for her ankle. I knew that was where she kept her backup gun strapped to her. She pulled the .357 magnum out and aimed it towards Tony.

"Mama, what in the hell are you doing?"

I was embarrassed.

She pushed me behind her.

"This man is a convicted rapist. I know him all too well."

I couldn't believe it when I saw a tear slip from her eye.

I looked over at Tony and he had his hands in the air.

"I don't know what you are talking about, but sadly you must have me mistaken with someone else. If you just put the gun down I'll go!"

"No nigger you stand right there, or I swear to God I'll blow your brains out."

I screamed.

"Oh my God mama what has gotten into you?"

"Roger Goodman, you don't remember me do you? My daughter was only five years old when you broke into our home and raped me by gun point? Remember that?"

Tony shook his head while holding his hands up. There was a look of fear in his eyes.

"Ma'am, my name is Tony Wallace. I have never raped a woman in my life. If you don't mind I'll just go now," he said fearfully.

"Liar, you are Roger Goodman!"

She lowered the gun towards his penis. I went for the gun. She wouldn't let go. Tony tried to intervene. A shot went off followed by two other shots. I stood still. The room was quiet. My mother dropped to her knees and Tony fell to the grown. Nathan was at the top of the stairs.

"Grandma? Mama?"

I looked around at the horrifying sight. My mother was holding her stomach. She had blood on her shirt. Tony had fallen to the ground. There was blood coming from his chest. I didn't know what to do. I had to think fast. My son was crying at the top of the stairs.

"Nathan, call 911 now!"

I waited until he disappeared. I was sure my mother was screaming from the way her mouth was opened, but I couldn't hear her. I looked at Tony and saw his mouth moving too, but no words were coming out. I couldn't figure out why I couldn't hear them. I tried not to panic. When I looked down there was a pool of blood on the floor. I grabbed the gun held in my mother's hand and placed it on the floor as I tried to help tend to her wound. She looked at me horrified.

"Amber, what the hell are you doing?"

Her voice sounded fuzzy. I was sure it was from the injury.

"I'm trying to help you mom you have been shot."

I looked over her body for the wound so I could stop the bleeding. I couldn't find it anywhere, but blood was everywhere.

"There is blood on your shirt mom, but I can't see where you have been shot."

She grabbed my hands.

"That's because I wasn't shot," she said a bit too quietly.

She had to be delirious. There was too much blood on the floor for her not to have gotten shot. I looked at her face and noticed her eyes were bloodshot red from crying and she still had that horrible look.

"Mom, don't try to talk the ambulance is on its way," I said. I was afraid I was going to lose my mother.

Suddenly, I felt a funny sensation course through my body. For some strange reason I began to get real cold. I felt myself slide down to the floor. There was a burning pain in my side. I put my hand by it and when I looked at my fingers they were covered in blood. My mother was right she hadn't been shot. It was me. I had been shot! The room started to blur and I could hear my mother screaming,

"Amber! Amber! Amber stay with me please, Oh Lord!" It sounded like she was twenty feet away instead of right in front of my face. I wanted to slap my mother for being so stupid, but the room went black before I could do anything.

Terrance

Today was the day of my daughter's funeral. I told Portia to have a small burial, because it was going to be hard seeing such a small child in a casket. I wasn't in the best health to attend, but I refused to miss it. My body had become weaker and I couldn't get around except by wheelchair, or nurse assistance. I had five, around the clock nurses at my home. Tanya came in and out to check on me, but our relationship just wasn't the same. I knew my wife loved me, but I also knew my illness was tearing us apart.

I was ready to go, ready to die.

Everyone had agreed to move into the house, but Tanya. I knew eventually she would. There was no need for me to stick around any longer. Tanya wanted Jason. I knew she did. He emailed me and told me about her phone call, and how hard it was for him to ignore her when she called. That let me know he had caught feelings. I wanted to give them my blessing to be together, but only after I died. I made sure I put it in my will how I felt.

One of the nurses walked into my room wearing her starch white uniform.

"Terrance, are you ready to go?"

What type of question is that? Is anyone ever ready to go to their child's funeral?

I wanted to scream and throw something, or better yet make someone feel all this pain I was feeling on a continued basis. I nodded my head not really wanting to face the world in this type of fashion. No one had ever seen Terrance Davenport like this. I stayed out of the spotlight once the cancer took over.

She and a male nurse helped me into a wheelchair. They guided me out to the hallway where several of my neighbors were standing in their doorways.

"Hang in there Terrance we are praying for your family," one neighbor said.

I nodded my head.

My other neighbor, Ana Maria, walked up to me placing her hand to my forehead.

"Hail Mary, full of grace. The Lord is with thee. Blessed art thou amongst women, and blessed is the fruit of thy womb, Jesus. Holy Mary, Mother of God, pray for us sinners, now and at the hour of our death. Amen!"

She touched my forehead, chest and shoulders making a cross symbol in the air.

It was a bit creepy how everyone was praying for me. I almost felt like it was my own funeral I was attending. The nurse wheeled me to the elevator and Ms. Lee was not too far behind. I heard the sound of her cane as it tapped the ground. She grabbed my hand and squeezed it.

"I love you Terrance!"

Tears welled up in my eyes and I smiled. She finally said my full name.

Tanya had left earlier. I told her to go ahead and ride in the limo along with my mom and dad. I didn't want Nathan to attend, but my mother felt otherwise and decided to bring him along. TJ had been released from the intensive care unit into my sister's care.

She was nine months pregnant, and since attending a funeral wasn't good for her unborn baby, she decided to stay home.

When we arrived at the Grace Chapel funeral home I didn't want to go in. I wasn't sure what it was, but funeral homes all had that funny smell. I don't know if it was the flowers or the embalming fluid, but either way it wasn't pleasant.

The parking lot was full of cars which I believe had to all belong to Portia's people. I watched from the backseat of the van as people emptied out of their cars and headed in to pay their respects. It looked like a mini ghetto fashion show. Some of the women had on short skirts and colorful stilettos, while some of the men had on three piece suits with matching hats, and shoes. Some were crying and others were hugging each other. I couldn't imagine how it would be when my time came.

Who would come to see me? Who would hold up my wife when she was down on her knees in grief? Would she even cry? Who would comfort my children?

It was such a sad occasion. I didn't want this for my daughter. She was only two years old. I remembered her as a quiet, but happy child. Half of these people probably didn't even know her.

"Terrance, they want to know if you would like to be wheeled in with the family."

Tanya had come up to the van and opened the door. She was dressed in a simple white, Chanel, pants suit. I knew the brand name, because I had bought it for her. Portia had asked everyone to wear white to the funeral instead of black.

Tanya looked like she had lost weight. Her once full figured frame looked more slender. I attributed that to the loss of our baby and the surgery she had on her appendix.

"Tell them I'll enter when I am good and ready," I said.

She gave me a look and walked away. Moments later a long, white, stretch limo, pulled up to the front doors of the funeral home. I knew it was Portia. She had a way of making an entrance no matter what it was. I watched as she got out from the back of the limo. She was wearing a tight low-cut black dress that stopped just above her knee, and sky high stilettos. She always had to stand out from the crowd. I just shook my head and watched as she and some of her friends went inside. I waited until I was sure all the screaming and shouting I knew she would be doing was done before I went in.

When the nurse wheeled me in, Tanya approached us and agreed to wheel me up to the tiny white casket with gold handles at the front of the funeral home. It was covered with a spray of white roses along with other flower arrangements surrounding it. I had never seen a casket that small. My heart sank.

"Are you ready?" Tanya asked.

Why the hell does everyone keep asking that dumb ass question?

I nodded my head. I don't think anyone could ever be prepared for seeing their child like this. I heard people crying and whispering as I passed the rows of chairs.

"That's Terrance Davenport, the baby's father," someone whispered.

"Oh dear lord, Terrance," someone else said.

I looked at the front row and noticed Portia was being rocked by her best friend Keisha, and her cousin Shavonne. A pair of dark Cartier sunglasses covered her eyes. Tanya stopped the wheelchair out of respect. I touched Portia's hand and held it for a moment. She gripped it back and began to cry.

"I'm sorry," she began to wail.

I patted her hand while choking down my tears.

I touched Tanya's hand and let her know I wanted to walk up to my daughters casket alone.

"Are you sure? I should get one of the male nurses just in case," she said.

She motioned for a nurse from the back of the chapel. He came and helped me stand up. I grabbed the cane he handed me and crept up to the casket. I looked inside at the motionless child lying against a white pillow. She had a smile on her ashen brown face that was a bit angelic. Her black curly hair was being held back by a white silk flowered head band. She was dressed in a white dress I had bought her for her first birthday. I touched her hand. It was small and cold to the touch. I felt the tears on my face as I held her hand in mine. I wished I had picked her up more and kissed her more often. All I had was a memory of her bright smile and her quiet nature that was much different from her mother's. My legs started to feel weak as the pain in my chest returned.

My babies were dead.

The thought of Tanya not being pregnant anymore, and the realization that my only daughter lay dead before me overwhelmed me. The tears spilled out onto her hand as I held her palm in mine.

"Daddy's sorry baby, I am so sorry I wasn't there to protect you."

The grief in my heart came rushing out. Tears poured down my face. I could no longer stand up. I held on to the casket, kissed my daughters forehead, and placed the picture I had of me holding her as an infant next to her side.

"Daddy will see you soon baby!" I whispered.

I tried to turn around and walk, but my emotions got the best of me. The nurse held on to me and helped me back to my wheelchair.

I heard Tanya cry out as a sudden grief overwhelmed her. I knew she was crying for our son. One of the chapel nurses caught her just before she hit the floor. I turned around to get back in my wheelchair so the pastor could start the service.

Pastor Michael Pitts delivered a very powerful sermon and afterwards there wasn't a dry eye in the house.

During the final procession, Portia got up from her seat, kicked off her shoes, and fell across the casket screaming and crying,

"Mommy's sorry baby, oh my God mommy's sorry! I'm sorry! God, I'm so sorry!"

It took three people to pull her off the casket. I was hurt just as much as she was, but her theatrics were a bit over the top. Just as the pallbearers were getting ready to move the casket someone was heard from the back yelling,

"Wait! Wait!"

I couldn't see who it was from where I was seated, but the voice sounded familiar. I heard gasps from the crowd, but still couldn't see the face.

"I have to see her just one time please!" The man said. There was obvious emotion in his voice.

"Why are you here?" Portia screamed.

"I'm tired of lying," the man said.

"Get him out of here!" Portia yelled.

"Do we need to call the police?" The chapel director asked me. I shrugged my shoulders not sure what was going on. My vision was still blocked, but I was sure of the familiarity of the person's voice.

"What is going on?" I asked Tanya.

She gave me a weird look and shrugged her shoulders.

I watched as some of Portia's family tried to restrain the person from coming to the front.

"Let me go!" He said.

"No just leave. You shouldn't be here right now!" I heard someone say.

"I have every right to be here," the man said.

"He sure does," Portia's mother said while standing up.

She moved near the man causing a scene and asked the people restraining him to let him go.

"You evil bitch why are you doing this?" Portia asked her mother.

I watched Cheryl move closer to her daughter before slapping her in the face.

"You are in the presence of the lord, have some respect, and you better watch who you are calling names girl. I am still your mother whether you like it or not," Cheryl said.

She reached for the man's hand to lead him to the casket. When he came into view I had to blink twice.

"Jason? What are you doing here I thought you were in Atlanta?" I asked.

He looked at me with eyes of sadness.

"I'm sorry man I should have told you, but I just found out," he said.

"Told me what?" I was curious to know what he had to say.

He looked at Portia and then back at me.

"Teyah is….," he paused.

"Dead, she's dead! Now let her rest in peace. Please!" Portia screamed out.

I looked over at Portia being held back by her friend Keisha. Jason walked closer to my wheelchair with tears in his eyes. He said,

"Teyah is my daughter man!"

I looked at him like he had three titties on his forehead.

"What the hell are you talking about she's your daughter?" I had no understanding.

He pulled out a piece of paper from his inside jacket pocket.

"I had my doubts so I had a DNA test done. They sent me the results last week when they performed the autopsy," he handed me the paper.

"He's a liar!" Portia screamed.

I ignored her and looked down at the paper in my hand. Amongst all the numbers on the page the one that stuck out the most was the 99.9% chance that he was indeed Teyah's father.

I felt like I was on an episode of the Maury show. I felt sick to my stomach. Here I was crying over a child that wasn't even mine. For the past two years I was led to believe that I had fathered Portia's second child when my best friend was the father.

"Portia, how could you? I gave this child my last name!" I looked at her.

I got up out of my wheelchair and tried to hobble my weak ass over to her to look her in the eyes.

"Terrance, let's just go," my father said. He and my brother Ty, had joined us at the front of the chapel.

I was beyond embarrassed and hurt.

"Why? Why would you betray me like that? Why didn't you just tell me he was her father?" I looked at Jason who was hanging his head. "And you! Man, you are my best friend. First you want to fuck my wife and now my daughter is really your daughter! You of all people could have been real with me!" I said.

I watched as Tanya's eyes increased in size. More gasps were heard from the crowd as people started talking. I turned to my brother who was standing on my left side.

"Get me out of here," I demanded. I glanced at the three of them standing there. "All of you can rot in hell!" My brother wheeled me out past Tanya, Portia and Jason who all remained inside the chapel.

Tanya

What the hell just happened?

We were at a funeral for my stepdaughter, who I found out is really not my stepdaughter, and the next minute Terrance is telling me to go to hell with Jason.

How did he know about us?

I knew I should have told him about our encounter.

The funeral ended very badly. Portia couldn't stop crying. I wasn't sure if that was because Terrance found out about Teyah not being his daughter, or if she was still hurt by her death. Jason wouldn't look at me at all. He paid his respects and left out just as quickly as he had come in. Everything had fallen apart in the blink of an eye. I didn't even want to go back home in fear of having to face Terrance, but I knew eventually I would have to. I decided to get in my BMW and go for a drive ending up at my sister's house.

"Hey sis what are you doing here? Aren't you supposed to be at a funeral?" She asked when she opened the door.

I walked into her living room and sat down on the couch.

"Girl, the funeral was a mess. Jason came in town and told everyone that Teyah was his daughter and he had the DNA results to prove it."

"What, get out of here? Where is Terrance?" she asked.

I dropped my head.

"Terrance told us all to go to hell and then he left with his family," I replied.

"Okay, so why didn't you leave with him?"

She looked at me for an answer. When I didn't respond she asked,

"Tanya, what did you do?"

I stared at my feet for a few seconds before looking into her burning gaze and responding.

"I let Jason perform oral sex on me and Terrance found out about it."

She shook her head.

"While I was pregnant," I added.

"Say what? Wow! That's low sis even for you, so now what?" She prodded.

"I don't know. Terrance won't talk to me. I tried to call his cell phone, but he sends me straight to voicemail. I tried sending him a text, but he isn't responding to that either. I know we are going to have to talk about it, but it's almost like for what. He's dying anyway and he hasn't made love to me in months," I was shocked at my own words.

Janine gave me an expression of pity as she joined me on the couch. We sat in silence for a moment until we were interrupted by a knock at the door. She got up to answer it.

"Jason Ellis, how are you? I haven't seen you in years," I heard my sister say.

My heart dropped at the mention of his name. *What was he doing here?* I quickly slipped into the kitchen to gather myself together. I found a glass in her cabinet and a bottle of water on the counter. I opened up the bottle of codeine in my purse and popped a pill in my mouth washing it down with the water.

"My sister must be in the bathroom or the kitchen I'll go find her." I heard Janine say as her footsteps grew closer.

She walked into the kitchen as I took a sip from my glass. She looked over at the prescription bottle in my hand. Her face dropped and she shook her head. There was an awkward moment of silence as I watched her try to think of what to say to me.

"Jason is here to see you."

I rolled my eyes and took another sip.

"I don't care tell him I'm not here," I replied.

Jason walked into the kitchen

"Now why would she tell me that when I can see that you are right here?" He asked.

I cut my eyes at Janine.

"Jason, how are you holding up?" I asked ignoring the fact that he looked damn good in his black Hugo Boss suit, with a fresh cut and shave.

"That's not what I came here to talk to you about." He moved closer to me. His fragrance permeated my nostrils.

"I'll just excuse myself and let you guys talk. I'll be in the living room watching TV if you need me," Janine said.

We watched as she made her exit out of the kitchen. Jason rushed over to me and kissed me on the lips. Reluctantly, I had to push him away.

"What the hell are you doing?" I asked.

"I missed you baby. Since you aren't pregnant with my friends baby any more, we can finish what we started a few months ago."

My body tingled at the memory of his tongue on my skin. Quickly, I cleared the thought from my head.

"Really, Jason? A few weeks ago you didn't want to talk to me, and you barely looked at me at the funeral. Now all of a sudden you miss me?"

He kissed me again this time I allowed him to linger for a second too long.

"Stop it!" I shoved him in his chest.

"Tanya, there is too much going on that I can't explain right now, but I missed you."

He reached his hand up to touch my face, but I smacked it away.

"Oh my goodness Tanya, come in here you have to see this!" Janine yelled to me from the living room. Jason followed behind me and hit me on my ass as we went to see what the fuss was about. I gave him a look while walking back into the living room where Janine was watching something on TV.

"Damn, isn't that Amber's mother?" Jason asked.

On the TV police were questioning neighbors and others about a shooting.

"Turn it up," I said.

"This morning deputy sheriff Lisa Sykowski shot and wounded two people inside of her home. One of the victims was a man by the name of Tony Wallace, and the other her own daughter, Amber Sykowski. Police say it was a case of mistaken identity. The sheriff said she went into another state of mind recalling a rape that happened over twenty-seven years ago, and thought Tony was the suspect that had raped her because he resembled her assailant. Her daughter, who was dating Tony Wallace, apparently tried to stop the altercation and was shot in the process. She is currently being treated for a gunshot wound to the abdomen. No word yet on her condition. Sheriff Sykowski has been suspended until the case undergoes further investigation. Stay tuned to Channel 12 for further news.

I couldn't believe my ears. I always knew Amber's mother was a bit off, but I never understood why.

"That would explain why Amber's mother is such a Looney tune," Jason said.

Janine and I turned and looked at him.

"Jason what do you want?" I asked.

Janine cut the volume down on the TV to hear his answer. He gave me a strange look and made a motion with his head towards the kitchen.

"Whatever you have to say to me you can say in front of my sister," I responded.

"Uh huh," Janine replied.

"Okay well it's like this since Terrance wanted to play the victim without my knowledge; I decided to come tell you what's really going on. He put me up to …you know," he stopped and made a hand gesture towards my hips.

I raised an eyebrow. He continued on,

"He gave me $25,000 the first time, but I turned it down. He then gave me another $20,000 and still I turned it down. Before I came back to Chicago and bumped into you at the store he offered me $60,000. He never told me he was sick or dying."

My heart dropped in the pit of my stomach. I couldn't believe what I was hearing.

"Did you take the money?" I asked trying hard to contain my anger. I had to know if he did what he did with me because he was paid to.

Jason was silent.

"Well did you?" Janine asked.

Jason nodded his head. I couldn't believe it! Then again maybe I could. What would a person truly do for $60,000? I think I was more hurt that Terrance put a wager on me than I was that Jason accepted it. My hurt began to turn back to anger.

"I was only supposed to do it one time and it was only because he couldn't satisfy you….." Jason said.

I cut him off midsentence.

"Get the fuck out!" I screamed.

Jason and Janine both looked at me.

"Get out! I don't want to see your face ever again. I thought you were my friend. How could you take money from my husband to perform oral sex on me? You had already gotten everything for free why didn't you tell him that, huh Jason?" I was livid.

I got up and hit him in his chest. All the anger and frustration over the past few months started coming out.

"I hate you! I hate you!" I screamed repeatedly as my fists pounded his chest. He seemed unaffected physically, but emotionally he looked hurt.

Janine came and pulled me away. Tears were falling uncontrollably down my face.

"Jason, I think its best that you go now," Janine said softly.

Jason had tears in his eyes.

"Tanya, it wasn't like that for me. I was wrong for taking the money, but I didn't take it just to sleep with you. I love you!"

"Jason, please just go," Janine pointed to the door.

Jason was hesitant to move. I watched as he opened his mouth to say something, but quickly thought about it and closed it. He shook his head, took one last look at me and headed towards the door.

When I heard the door close I fell to my knees. I couldn't figure out what I had done in my life to have to suffer through all of this pain. I loved Terrance unconditionally, but there was no way I was going to let him continue to break down my life because he was losing his own.

Portia

After burying my baby girl and the fiasco Jason created, I no longer wanted to be in Chicago. There were just too many negative memories around reminding me of everything I wanted to forget. I never thought he would come to Teyah's funeral and reveal the secret I held on to for two years. I always knew eventually I would have to face my demons, but I assumed I had time.

I had slept with Jason on a humbug. It wasn't even good sex. It was pity sex. I was crying about not having a man in my life because I was still in love with Terrance, and Jason was whining about some chic that had cheated on him. We both had a few drinks and my panties fell off. The sexual episode ended in less than twenty minutes.

I had sex with Terrance two nights later, and when I found out I was pregnant I prayed every day that it was his. When I finally gave birth I knew there was no way in hell my baby could belong to Terrance. She came out light skinned with no freckles and a small forehead. Nathan was the only light skinned child he had and that was because Amber was white. When he questioned Teyah's skin color, I fed him some bullshit about looking like me when I was little and how she was probably picking up the skin color from my family line. I just couldn't tell him the truth. Besides, the look on Tanya's face when she found out I was carrying another child by Terrance was priceless. I vowed to never tell anyone, but somehow Jason figured it out. I wish I knew he had gone and took that damn DNA test.

My court date was coming up on Monday to determine what type of sentencing the judge would give to me for this child endangerment and neglect case.

My attorneys were working it out to have me put on probation. Cheryl, filed a claim for temporary custody of TJ until my sentencing, and despite the negative backlash from Terrance's parents, she won.

Sometimes I wish I had never met Terrance Davenport. I would never have touched a bottle had it not been for his bullshit, and maybe I would be a better person.

According to the agreement I signed I had to attend an AA meeting. I was on my way to my first meeting being driven there by Keisha like I was some child.

"You know I could have driven myself. I'm not handicapped," I told her.

"I want to make sure you are going to keep your end of the bargain," she said to me.

I rolled my eyes. I surely did not feel like sitting amongst a bunch of alcoholics crying their eyes out over their fucked up lives. I had done enough crying for an entire army over the past few days.

We pulled up to a brown unmarked, brick building. The parking lot was already full of cars and people were going inside.

"Okay here you are. I will be out here waiting when you are done," she pushed the button to unlock the doors.

I looked at Keisha like she was crazy.

"Okay mom did you pack my lunch too?" I asked.

She gave me a smile as I got out of the car. I hesitated walking through the doors not wanting to face the reality of being labeled as an alcoholic. I wanted a drink right now.

A short chubby lady opened the door for me and smiled.

"Hello, come right on in we are happy to have you here," she said cheerfully.

"Shit, not as happy as I would be if I had a drink," I mumbled.

"I'm sorry did you say something?" She asked.

"I said hello and thank you."

She gave me half of a smile and said,

"You are very welcome. Just go down that hall and turn left into the room with the green door."

I walked in feeling like a kid on the first day of school. The hallways were lit with fluorescent lights and were painted a crappy cream color, and had pictures of people smiling and shaking hands with other people. On the wall to my left, the words *"Right this way to a different you"* were painted boldly in green above an arrow pointing me in the direction I needed to go.

Upon entering, I noticed the room was a bright yellow, with multi colored chairs lined up in a perfect circle. There were about eleven other people standing around talking to one another. One woman with micro braids down her back approached me with her hand out and smiled.

"Hello my name is Marlena, but everyone just calls me Lena. Welcome to the twelve step program. Grab a seat and we will get started shortly."

She pointed to one of the hideous colored chairs.

All this extra happy friendly bullshit was making me sick to my stomach. I found a seat away from the circle in the back near an older white man who looked the way I felt, tired!

I looked around at some of the people in the room and wondered if they were all alcoholics. There was a young man with dreads, who looked to be about twenty-one years old wearing white skinny jeans, a black v-neck t-shirt, with a black and white scarf around his neck. There was another man sitting in the circle who looked like he was in his late seventies wearing brown corduroy pants, and a tweed jacket with some brown dress shoes. Two of the women next to him were overweight and looked like they were middle aged forties.

There was another woman who looked my age, but I wasn't sure because of all the makeup she had caked on her face. The woman, who introduced herself to me earlier as Lena, walked into the room and closed the door behind her.

"Welcome again everyone. I want to let you know that this program is going to leave you motivated and uplifted to change your lives. The only requirement for membership is a desire to stop drinking. There are no dues for AA membership we are self-supporting through our own donations. Our primary purpose is to stay sober and help other alcoholics to achieve sobriety," she said with that damn smile on her face.

"What if I'm drunk right now?" The young man asked.

I giggled.

"Then you don't need to be here," the older man with the corduroy pants said.

Lena gave the young man a look before responding,

"We would like you all to be serious when you attend the meetings. The purpose is for us to help you to attain sobriety. You have to take the first step. Why don't we go ahead and have everyone introduce themselves. I see some new faces today."

She looked right at me. This felt like being at a new church when the pastor asked you to stand up and introduce yourself. I tried to shrink down in my seat so that no one would notice me but that was impossible.

"We will start with you Christian; introduce yourself to the others so they will know how it works." Lena pointed to the man sitting next to me. The older man cleared his throat and stood up. He walked over to the circle of chairs.

"My name is Christian Smith and I am an alcoholic. I have been sober for 120 days and counting," he said proudly.

In unison Lena and her assistant, the chubby lady, replied,

"Hi Christian!"

I shook my head.

This is some bullshit.

I picked up my Gucci bag from off the seat of the chair next to me and stood up to leave.

"And you are?" Lena asked me.

Now everyone's attention was directed towards me.

"Please come to the circle and tell us your name," she said pointing to the chairs.

"I am leaving that's who I am," I made my way towards the door.

"Why? You think you too good to be here with us Ms. Fancy boots?" The young boy said to me.

"Those boots are cute girl," someone said referring to my Gucci boots I had on.

"This is your first day right? Ms......" Lena was waiting on me to answer.

"Didn't you hear me? I am leaving. I am too good for this! I am not an alcoholic just because I like having a drink or two. You people have issues," I turned once again to leave.

"I bet you are one of those girls who carry those little mini bottles of alcohol in her purse, or has her own personal flask. Maybe, you even have liters of cheap brands under your sink for when you can't make it to the bar," a black lady said.

I thought about my collection of Vodka under my kitchen sink.

"You don't know me," I said to her through gritted teeth.

I was getting upset.

"Leave Ms. Fancy boots alone. She is not an alcoholic she just likes to drink too much sometimes," someone else said.

Some of them laughed.

Lena looked at me for a reaction. I had reason to believe she was allowing this to happen on purpose.

I rolled my eyes as hard as I could and flipped my hair weave over my shoulder.

"Like I said I am *not* an alcoholic!"

"Well then why the hell are you in here wasting our time? See we are alcoholics! We have lost family members over this shit. Some of us have been arrested for DUI's, car accidents, been hospitalized for alcohol poisoning, and others have bottomed out spending their last few dollars to get a drink. Oh but not you, you have your $1500 boots and your $800 purse and maybe you like to take a drink or two here and there. You are so much better than the rest of us," a white lady said to me.

I glared at her.

Lena stood up.

"Okay guys that's enough. If she feels she doesn't belong here then that's her right. I do want to say that I have yet to meet a person who walks through that green door who doesn't have a story to tell." She looked at me.

I felt everyone's eyes were on me. I should have walked out the first time I had gotten up out of my seat. I thought about my daughter and my son and the tears came to my eyes. I moved to the circle and set my purse down in the chair. I let out a big sigh before deciding to tell them who I was.

"My name is Portia.....Portia Jackson and as much as I feel that I am not an alcoholic, I am! I have only been sober for a couple of weeks and that's because I had to bury my two year old daughter who lost her life behind my drinking." Fresh tears fell from my eyes. I could see heads shaking in pity.

Lena came next to me hugged me, and put her arm around my shoulder.

"Welcome Portia. Everyone say hello to Portia."

"Hi Portia," they said in chorus.

I proceeded to tell them my story and felt better when I revealed to them the reasons behind my drinking. I learned I wasn't drinking because of Terrance; I was drinking to numb the pain of all the things I had experienced in my life. After listening to the things everyone talked about, I realized I was no different than any of them. We all had a major problem and that was trying to drown out the issues in our lives with alcohol.

When the meeting was over I felt drained. I cried listening to some of the stories of people abusing their loved ones or doing any and everything to get a drink. It was like a drug only in liquid form.

As I was walking towards the exit, Alice, the white lady who fronted on me earlier, approached me.

"Portia, I want to apologize for calling you out. It's just I look at you and I see me. Although you are black and I'm white." She laughed. "I used to be young and fancy free chasing after a man with money, because I felt he owed me since I had his children. My drinking began the same way. I was trying to drown out the fact he married someone else. I just want you to know that I truly understand what you are feeling right now, and if you ever feel yourself slipping give me a call."

She smiled and handed me a piece of paper with her number on it. I saw Lena in the background smiling.

"Thank you Alice," I said. She gave me a hug. Immediately, I stiffened at her touch, but then relaxed.

I made my way back down the hall and out the door to where Keisha was waiting for me.

"How did it go?" She asked.

"It was okay!"

She gave me a look as if she was trying to read my thoughts.

"Just okay?"

"Yea, just okay." I paused. "I think I am going to keep going. I think being here with others like me might help me sort out some of my issues I have," I said.

She smiled and hugged me.

Why is everyone in such a hugging mood today?

When I looked at her there were tears in her eyes.

"Portia, I really do hope this helps you. I have had to stand by and helplessly watch you tear yourself apart over the past few years. I knew when Teyah died," She stopped choking down tears. "I knew I had to intervene in some way. What kind of friend would I be if I didn't?"

I grabbed her hand.

"Thank you Keisha, for everything." She smiled and we got into her Lexus parked by the curb. She drove off and I remained silent with the thoughts of changing my life swimming around in my head.

Amber

I looked around the hospital room I was in listening to the sound of the machines beeping in my ear. I tried to sit up but felt a tremendous amount of pain in my side. My mouth was dry and my legs felt heavy. When I looked to my left Tony was staring at me.

"Hey beautiful you're awake," he said.

He had a large bandage across his shoulder and his shirt had dried blood on it.

I tried to move my hand and felt a twinge of pain from an IV that was stuck inside of it. I couldn't talk because of a tube that was shoved in my nose and down my throat. I pulled at it so I could ask Tony a question but ended up choking.

"Hang on I'll get a nurse to get that out."

He left the room and returned moments later with a nurse.

"Glad to see you awake Ms. Sykowski. I need you to take a deep breath while I pull this tube out okay? On the count of three…one, two, three." She pulled gently on the long tube.

I felt it as it seemed to travel out of my stomach as it slid up my throat and out of my mouth. I coughed and gagged. She handed me a cup of water.I felt like I had been on a desert and this was the first drop of water I had received.

"Drink slowly," the nurse advised. When I was done she took the cup from me and began to check my vitals. Hoarsely I asked,

"Tony what are you doing here?"

Tony gave me a weak smile and rubbed my hair. I watched the dark skinned nurse make notes on my chart before she answered for him,

"Honey, be thankful he is here. He only had a minor wound compared to yours. He has been by your side for the past three nights. I'd say he's a keeper." She smiled at the both of us. I looked over at Tony this time really looking at him. He looked tired and he had small bags underneath his eyes.

"I can't remember what happened," I said.

I stared at the big bandage on his shoulder.

He started laughing.

"Your mother shot me that is what happened."

Did he just say my mother shot him?

"What?" I asked in disbelief.

He nodded his head. I tried to recall the events that happened, but my thoughts were cloudy. Tony filled in the missing pieces.

"She shot me because she thought I was the man who raped her twenty-seven years ago. If you had not of stepped in and tried to save me she might have killed me." He looked out the window fighting back emotion.

"Wait, my mother was raped? I don't understand."

Tony was about to say something, but he was stopped by someone else.

"I don't either. I'm so sorry this happened to you, Amber," a man's voice said.

It was my father. I watched him as he walked in the room. He must have been standing in the doorway.

"Daddy?"

"I should leave you two alone," Tony said as he got up.

"No don't go," I pleaded. Any man who stayed by my side after my mother shot him was someone I didn't want to lose.

I touched his hand. He smiled.

"I'm going to walk down to the cafeteria to get a bite to eat," Tony said.

He kissed my forehead. I really needed to know what happened especially with my father being here. He didn't show his face in public very often. He was always working or away on some business meeting, so I didn't get to see much of him. That was how most of my life went. He waited until Tony left the room. I looked my dad over drinking in his presence. He was wearing a three piece Brooks Brother's navy colored suit with matching shirt and tie.

He pulled up a chair and sat down next to my bed.

"How are you feeling love?" He asked.

"Confused, and in pain." I told him.

He took a deep breath before he responded.

"I guess I need to tell you what should have been told to you years ago. Your mother wasn't raped! That is what she told the media and me for that matter until I investigated the case myself. Twenty seven years ago she had an affair with an African American man by the name of Roger Goodman. You were five years old. I was away at a business meeting and we had a big argument because she was tired of staying at home with you. I called her a bad mother for always wanting to leave you. She met Roger months earlier at one of my business conventions I took her to, and they kept in touch through emails and phone calls. The more time I was away it turned into short visits and hotel rooms. I assume when she started to fall in love he decided to leave her alone and go back to his wife and kids. Your mother can't take rejection from any source so she went after him and tried to physically harm him. He was going to turn her in, but since she was a police officer at that time he decided it was his word against hers. She turned it into a spectacle and accused that man of rape. His wife left him, taking the kids with her, and he ended up committing suicide before he could serve any time in prison. Your mother never got over his death and turned her anger to every black man she saw."

I was speechless. My mother didn't want me dating black men and now I understood why, she couldn't have one for herself!

"I'm sorry you and your friend were injured behind this madness. I feel like it's my fault. I knew she needed help, but I was just disgusted at the fact that she cheated on me during a time when I needed her most. Instead of me leaving, I turned my back and hid behind my work. I never meant for you to get hurt."

"It's not your fault daddy," I said placing my hand on his.

My father truly looked sad. He held on to my hand and we sat in silence until Tony returned to the room.

I was released from the hospital a couple of days later and Tony and his friend moved all of my things into the new house. Nathan was staying with Terrance's parents until I settled in comfortably.

I steered clear of my mother and only went back to her house when she was gone. I would forgive her for shooting me, but I couldn't forgive her just yet for making my life hell, because of what she couldn't have. My relationship with Terrance might have been a lot different if she hadn't of interfered.

I asked Rebecca to stay with me a couple of nights until I got used to being in such a big house.

"Girl this house is awesome! I just took a bath in that big Jacuzzi bath tub you have in your room. Your closet is humongous! I could move in it and you would never even know I was here," Becky said.

I laughed.

"You should be used to living like this Ms. High power attorney," I said to her.

"True, but my money isn't long enough for all these luxuries. Terrance really made sure to take care of you. He has you covered. Do you read your mail at all?"

She handed me a piece of mail that had been opened.

"Becky, come on you are an attorney you know the law. Why did you open my mail?"

"I am your attorney and I had to make sure Terrance wasn't pulling a fast one on you," she said.

I looked at the paper. It was my bank statement. Terrance made good on part of his offer and deposited over $500,000 in my account.

"I don't get it. I thought we all had to agree to move in before he gave us anything. I don't think Tanya and Portia agreed to move in yet," I said.

Becky was looking out the floor to ceiling window.

"The view is awesome you can see Lake Michigan from here," she said.

"Becky, are you listening to me?"

She turned around.

"Who cares about what the others agreed to do or not do. You have half a million dollars versus that $50 you had before so shut up and go spoil yourself a little bit. Get your nails and hair done. Do something different for a change. Color your hair or something. You have more money than me now."

I thought about it. I hadn't been to a beauty salon in years and my nails could use a manicure. I called the bank to verify the balance and they confirmed it. Becky and I decided to have a spa day and get our nails, toes and hair done. For the first time in a long time I was able to pay for everything. Although my parents had money it was just that, *their* money. This money Terrance gave me was mine and I didn't have to answer to anyone for it.

Once we were done, we had lunch at a small café, and went shopping on the popular Magnificent Mile which was Michigan Avenue. Upon arriving back at the house I noticed an unfamiliar car parked in the driveway.

"Are you expecting company?" Becky asked.

"No. No one knows I moved here, but you Tony and Terrance."

The closer we got to the house we noticed a person getting out of the car.

"Oh lord its Portia," I told Becky.

Portia looked oddly different. She had on a regular pair of jeans, a loose fitting black t-shirt, and tennis shoes. Her hair was even different. She was a far cry from her normal attire. When I looked at her she was staring at the house. Becky jumped out the car and walked right up on her.

"If you think you are about to bring that ghetto drama to my friend think again sweetie! Don't let the bougie fool you. This white girl was raised on the South Side of Chicago," Becky said.

Portia turned around and started clapping.

"Great performance, but I am not here on any ghetto drama as you say. I am moving in today and I beat the moving truck here. I'm just waiting on my stuff," she said.

Becky looked at me curiously. I shrugged my shoulders. I had no idea she was moving in. I thought she was going to jail since she still had yet to be sentenced.

"Well, welcome home I guess," I said feeling stupid after I said it. This would never be home if Portia was here. That is when reality had finally hit that I was going to be sharing a house with my arch enemy.

We entered the house and I put my shopping bags in the empty living room. I couldn't help but to notice Portia looked sad.

"Are you okay?" I felt obligated to ask.

"No, I'm not but I will be. I miss my kids. I have to have a stable living arrangement and maintain sobriety for six months before they will release TJ in my care. My mother is fighting hard for permanent custody," she said while looking vulnerable and defeated.

I had never seen this side of Portia so it caught me off guard. She was really sad.

"I'm sorry to hear that," was all I could manage to say.

Rebecca made a noise, rolled her eyes and walked to the enormous kitchen leaving us alone in the foyer.

"Well I had a long day. I'm going to go and chill in my room. If you need anything until your stuff gets here just let me know," I said before walking up the spiral staircase.

Portia nodded her head and I retreated to my room.

"This might not be so bad after all," I said to Becky who was eating popcorn and flipping through channels on the 72 inch flat screen TV hoisted up on the wall in my bedroom.

She shook her head and rolled her eyes again turning her attention back to the television.

Later on that night as I was coming from the kitchen I heard Portia crying softly and my heart dropped. She cried out for her daughter over and over and the words "mommy's sorry" was all she kept saying. Maybe she wasn't the devil after all.

Maybe.

Terrance

I hadn't spoken to my wife since the day of Teyah's funeral which was exactly three weeks ago today. I heard she was staying at her sister's house. I knew I had to stop ignoring her phone calls and emails, but I just couldn't face what was revealed at the funeral. I knew she would question me about how I knew her and Jason had a sexual encounter. I'm sure Jason told her I paid him and that would make her furious.

Amber and Portia had finally moved into the house. I wasn't sure how much longer I was going to be able to hang on, so I went ahead and purchased the house in case they all changed their minds. My health was deteriorating more rapidly. Tanya was supposed to come by today and pick up some papers. I was going to try and talk to her.

I heard the nurse talking to her when she came in. I pressed the call button on my bed to alert the nurse I needed something. She came in right away.

"Yes Terrance," she said.

Damn she was fine.

Even in her nurse uniform this nurse had ass for days and curves that I wouldn't mind taking a ride on. She reminded me of a thicker version of that actress Nia Long.

I ain't dead yet.

I tried to focus on her face and not her body.

"Can you please have Tanya come in here?" I asked her. I watched as her butt clapped underneath her pants when she walked away.

193

A few seconds later Tanya appeared in the doorway.

"What?" She said.

I wasn't used to hearing her use such a brash tone with me. I looked her over and noticed she had lost even more weight. Her hair was in a ponytail, her skin was dry, and she was wearing a green jogging suit that did nothing for her figure.

"Well, hello to you too wife," I said.

"I want a divorce!" She said as if she had been holding in the words all day. She looked surprised when she said it.

I assumed this was about Jason.

Keeping the hurt out of my voice I responded dryly,

"For what, I'll be gone soon and you won't have to worry about me."

She stopped and gave me a long hard stare before shaking her head.

"Terrance, I am so sick and tired of you trying to use your sickness as a way of not dealing with anything. You have been doing nothing but throwing your control around with it. You want to control your kid's mothers with money and make them move into one house. You want to control my sex life by paying Jason to sleep with me. You want to control every fucking thing. I am tired of it! I don't want your damn money! I could take it all if I wanted to anyway!"

Clearly, she was upset. I tried a soft approach.

"Tanya, baby, I don't want to end it like this."

"Well what do you prefer? I am done waiting on you to die. I am done waiting to live. I want to be free. Let me go Terrance so I can live my life without you." She began to cry.

I was hurt. That was not something I ever wanted to hear my wife say. I had no words.

She wiped her eyes.

"I just came to get some of my things," Tanya said as she moved around the room.

She stopped when she came to our wedding picture on the wall.

"What am I doing?" I heard her whisper out loud. She shook her head and looked at me.

The pain in my chest was heavy and felt like someone was trying to tear my heart out. I wasn't sure if it was the cancer, or my broken heart that was causing so much pain.

"If a divorce is what you want I will give you that," I managed to say.

She continued to look at me.

"Terrance, I am just dealing with a lot of emotions right now. Some days are harder for me than others. I miss you. I miss us. I miss how much fun we used to have before this disease took over. I miss laughing and playing. I miss making love to you and you making love to me. God, how I miss that the most! I miss you always being there for me and now when it's my turn to be there for you I'm failing at it," she dropped her head and started crying again

The pain in my chest grew a bit stronger.

"Tanya I love you. I always will. I never meant to cause any pain. If I could go back and undo all of this mess I would. I miss you too. Do you know how hard it was asking, no paying, and my best friend to sleep with you so you could be satisfied? That shit was hard! You will never understand how hard that was for me. I just want you and my kids to be happy."

There was silence in the room and I noticed the figure standing in the corner with an open palm reaching out to me. I had to be going crazy because there was no one else in the room but Tanya and I.

"I think it's time for me to go," I whispered.

"What? No Terrance, no, not yet!"

The pain in my chest grew stronger this time cutting my airway. I could barely breathe. The person in that corner came closer reaching out a hand visible to only me. I was delusional. It surely wasn't Jesus.

"Terrance, stay with me don't you leave me now!"

I could hear Tanya's voice but I couldn't respond. I felt cold, lightheaded and dizzy all at the same time. The walls felt like they were closing in at a rapid speed. I saw my life as a toddler and then as a teenage boy playing outside on the basketball courts. I saw my wedding day at the courthouse and my sons faces as they burst into the world out of their mothers vaginas. I saw my mother laughing and crying and who I thought was my daughter taking her first steps. I saw me at school and then I saw myself alone in a dark room.

It was cold and very quiet. Was I dead? Is this what death really felt like? The room grew colder. I could see the nurse moving as she pumped her hand on my chest. I knew Tanya was screaming in the corner because her mouth was open and the expression on her face was one of terror, but I couldn't hear her. All I could see was movement, no sound. I wanted a second chance. A second chance to correct the wrongs, to hold my kids, to make love to my wife, to tell my parents I loved them.

But it was too late.

My time had come and there wasn't a damn thing I could do to stop it!

Tanya

I fell to my knees as the pounding of my heart beat rapidly against my chest. I watched the nurse as she tried to revive Terrance over and over. She had to call in another nurse for help. I stood by helplessly watching as they pumped Terrance's chest and checked his pulse.

"We are going to have to put him on life support before we lose him," the nurse said to me.

I had no words I just stood there staring. The nurses looked at each other and started moving around quickly grabbing items and pushing machines into the room.

"Tanya, this is a respirator that will breathe for Terrance until he breathes on his own or until you ….until you sign the form to shut it off and…let him go," she said softly. She pointed at the machine with the accordion like thing attached to it.

The older nurse walked over to where I was sitting. She touched my shoulder gently.

"Honey, this is the final step. I will call the doctor and let him know. He might want to come by and check Terrance's rate of progression. This is the time to call any family and start making your arrangements," she said softly.

I had no words. I couldn't move. I felt numb. I knew it was coming, but I just didn't know when. This was it. *The final step* the nurse said. I knew it. I just couldn't come to terms with it. There were tubes coming out of his mouth and nose, and he looked almost peaceful if it weren't for all the stuff in the way.

I didn't even tell him I loved him. I didn't even get to say goodbye. The only man I ever loved besides my father was leaving me.

I needed something.

I watched as they hooked up a brain wave activity monitor to him. *Where was my bottle of pills?* I needed to ease the pain filling up inside of me?

I should have never told him I wanted a divorce. *Oh God those were my last words to him. He will die knowing I was angry.*

I was feeling guilty. I laid on the floor watching and listening as the machine went up and down.

"Tanya, I spoke with the doctor and he is on his way over to evaluate Terrance's condition. If you need me to call someone to be here with you I can," she said while looking at me for a response.

I looked up at the nurse that had been at my husband's side for the past few months. She was a white older woman with gray strands scattered through her brown hair. Her voice was soothing and pleasant as she talked.

"I should have never quit my nursing job. I would have been more of a help to him. When I got pregnant he said I didn't have to work anymore," I said out loud while staring at the wall.

The nurse looked at me with concern.

"Your sister Janine, is her number still on the fridge?" She asked.

I didn't respond to the nurse's question. My eyes went back to the bed where Terrance laid. I stared at his hands. Big, strong, hands he used to caress my face with and hold me tight in his arms. *Who was going to hold me now? Who would touch my face and tell me how beautiful I was?* The nurse walked away from me and whispered something to the other nurse standing at the doorway. She approached me. She was tall, skinny and black reminding me of the model Naomi Campbell in the face.

"Tanya dear, I'm going to check your vitals okay?"

She pulled the stethoscope from around her neck and put it to my chest.

I started to laugh. I recalled the time in college when I had purposely wore a skirt so that Terrance would notice me. It happened to be really windy that day and I took my fat ass outside where he was playing basketball after school. The wind caught my skirt and blew it right up showing the world my white grandma panties. It was the same day I didn't realize I had started my period. Everyone who was anyone seemed like they had all witnessed that moment and started laughing and pointing at me. I was so embarrassed, but Terrance being the gentleman he was ran over and gave me his jacket.

I continued laughing until my tears snuck in and turned me into a crying, bubbling idiot. It felt like someone was trying to rip my stomach out. Snot was running out of my nose dripping down on my breasts. I felt an anxiety attack creeping in on me. I hadn't had an episode since after my mother died years ago. I missed my mom. She would know what to do in this situation. She would hold my hand and sit with me until I was okay. She would rub my hair and pull my head to her chest to comfort me. I began to sweat profusely and my breathing was shallow. I started rocking back and forth.

"Tanya, you have to breathe slowly," I heard the nurse say to me.

I shook my head. I didn't want to breathe. First my mother, then my baby, now my husband, death was not my friend. It hated me. It had taken away the people I loved more than anything in the world. I wanted to die. I wanted to experience this pain no more.

"Gladys, I need your help in here. She is starting to hyperventilate. Tanya, come on you have to take slow, deep breaths," the nurse instructed.

I heard the nurse telling me to breathe, but I didn't want to. I wanted to be with Terrance. *Have you ever loved someone so much you want to die for them?*

No one can ever understand that. They would just say I was crazy, or stupid for trying to die for a man who did the shit Terrance did to me.

I saw the doctor enter the room. He checked over Terrance, wrote some things down on his chart, and then knelt down beside me on the floor.

"Tanya, do you remember me? I am Dr. Lawrence. I need you to listen to my voice and follow my instructions okay?"

I couldn't understand why everyone was talking to me like a baby. I understood every word they were saying, I just didn't want to do what they were telling me. I felt a tingling in my hands that began to travel to my arms. The doctor flashed a light in my eyes.

"How long has she been like this?" He asked the nurses in the room.

"About twenty minutes now. She just started sweating and rocking shortly before you got here," the older nurse responded.

"Did you check her vitals?" The doctor asked.

"Yes doctor, her pulsox is 120 and her BP is 140 over 95,"said the skinny nurse.

"Okay, we need to get her to calm down before she sends herself into cardiac arrest. Is there anyone we could call that she knows?"

"Her sister Janine was unreachable, but I called two other numbers listed for a Portia and Amber. Portia is the only one available and said she was on her way over," the nurse said.

"Okay good. I'll try to get her calm until then," the doctor said.

Why is everyone talking about me like I am not sitting right here? Did they just say that bitch Portia was on her way over? I know I am about to die now. She would love to sit and watch me go through this, or try to kill me herself.

"She's not responding to me so I'm going to have to give her something." I watched as the doctor made movements toward me and stuck me in my leg with a needle. I didn't even flinch.

I don't know what the doctor gave me, but it sure has me floating. I think he gave me too much, because I can see Portia has now entered the room wearing a pair of denim jeans, a t-shirt, and tennis shoes. She looks normal. No makeup and no weave. That isn't right at all. She is supposed to look like she is ready to have her picture taken. She always has on something too tight and some type of stilettos with a matching purse. That's the Portia I know. I don't know who this other plain bitch is.

I watched her look over at Terrance with a pained expression on her face. I knew she loved my husband. She still does its written on her face. I need to get up. I need to leave this scene. When I tried to stand I met the floor face first and the room went completely black.

Portia

When I got the call from Terrance's nurse I was sitting in the backyard staring at the pool. I missed my children and so desperately wanted a drink. I was now thirty days sober. It was very difficult. Amber took all of the wine in the house and hid it in her room which she kept locked. I know because I checked. She didn't own anything of value to me except those glass bottles of Merlot, Chardonnay, and Moscato she had. Living with her wasn't too bad. We both kept our distance. I would go to my room which was too big for one person and stay there watching TV or sit in my closet on the floor. Keisha would come by from time to time to take me to my AA meetings, but she had grown distant in our friendship. I don't blame her. I had too much time to think about all the things I had done over the years and all the hurt I had caused.

Living in this house felt like a type of prison. I almost think Terrance wanted it to be that way.

We were prisoners of our own mistakes and he was the guard. I was able to visit with TJ on the weekends, but only under supervision. He still wasn't allowed to be left alone in my care.

The nurse on the phone explained to me about Terrance being put on life support and Tanya's actions. She told me they needed someone to come and try to calm Tanya down. I found it funny the nurse asked me of all people to come by. I looked around before finally agreeing that I would. *Who would have ever thought it would be me trying to calm my baby daddy's, wife down from the ledge of her demise?*

I laughed out loud.

I called my friend to tell her the news and to ask her for a ride. I didn't want to drive my car over there by myself.

"Hey Keisha I need a ride to Terrance's house."

"For what?" Keisha asked.

"Tanya is over there going crazy and they tried to reach her sister and Terrance's parents, but no one is answering."

"So they called you?" The tone in her voice was comical.

"Yea, it sounds crazy right?"

"Crazy isn't the word try delusional, retarded, ludicrous, and insane," Keisha added.

"Well damn I know I ain't that bad."

"Girl please, you and Tanya trying to save each other is like batman and the joker being friends. I suppose this is your time to do a good deed. I'll be by shortly," Keisha said before hanging up.

I threw on a pair of Levi jeans, a t-shirt laying on my floor, and my Nikes. Although my closet was full of designer clothes I didn't even have the energy to get dressed up anymore. I took my sew-in out a week ago and decided to wear my natural hair for a change.

When I arrived to Terrance's apartment the nurse buzzed me in. I walked down the hall and bumped in to his old neighbor, Ms. Lee who lived a couple of doors down from them.

"Excuse you hussy," she said to me.

I looked at her and frowned.

"Yes I'm talking to you with your tramp ass. You shouldn't be here. They are dealing with enough as it is and here you go coming to cause more trouble. "

"I'm sorry," was all I could manage to say before I walked away from her.

Seems like it was the only two words I had been using consistently lately. I hesitated at the door.

Maybe I should turn around. Who was I to help Tanya?

Before I could change my mind the nurse opened the door. I walked inside and caught a cold chill. The air inside was certainly different than before. She led me through the burgundy colored hallway with the expensive paintings on the wall. We crossed the living room and passed a room that housed a stark white sofa and love seat combination with red accents.

I never noticed this room before. I guess Tanya does have some taste.

The nurse cleared her throat when she noticed me standing in the middle of the room. I continued to follow her through the dining room leading to the room Terrance was in. I assumed it used to be a den until Terrance took ill, now the room looked like a makeshift hospital room.

There were different types of machines and monitors throughout the room. The flat screen that hung on the wall was now functioning as a gigantic monitor. Terrance was lying still in the bed, hooked up to all different kinds of machines.

One was recording his heart, another charting his brain activity, and another machine controlled his breathing. When I looked to my left, Tanya was slumped over in a corner with the doctor holding an oxygen mask up to her face. She was drenched in sweat and her skin looked pale.

"Hi, I'm Portia," I said to the doctor.

"Great, hold this up to her face and try to talk to her. I gave her some medicine to stop the anxiety attack, but she really needs a friend," he said before walking away.

A friend! What an understatement. What type of friend could I be to someone who disliked me just as much as I disliked them? Tanya's eyes grew wide as she tried to stand up to get away from me. She stood to her feet and went crashing right back down to the floor. I assumed she knocked herself unconscious from the way her head hit the floor.

"We need to move her to her bedroom. Portia can you help us?" The nurse asked.

I gave a small laugh.

This just keeps getting better and better. Now I have to help carry this bitch to her room?

The nurses and I picked Tanya up from the floor with me holding her arms, one nurse holding her legs, and the other supporting the middle of her body.

I should drop her on her head and leave her here.

"Portia, can you hold her up a little bit more? You are going to cause us to drop her on her head," the nurse said to me as if she could read my thoughts.

We finally got her into her bedroom and laid her across the humongous bed. I sat on the mini couch in front of her bed waiting for her to regain consciousness.

Wow, she has a damn couch in her bedroom. Ugh, maybe I shouldn't be sitting on it no telling what they have done on it.

I jumped up and took a look around the room. There was a huge picture of Tanya and Terrance naked with only their private parts covered, laying on a bear skin rug, both of them gazing at each other sensually.

Ugh. I did not want to see Tanya in all her glory. Bitch still don't have shit on me. I got more ass than she does, and my titties look much better than those small oranges she has on her chest.

I couldn't get past the way Terrance was looking at her. His look was filled with desire, lust and most importantly….love! He never looked at me like that. I guess I was always jealous, because I wanted that same happiness she had found. I knew there was a point in my life that I would have to let go of the notion of Terrance ever leaving Tanya to be with me. He only used me for sex and I had latched on to that need with everything I had. In the end Keisha was right it was Tanya that had everything.

Tanya's foot moved as she started to come to. She opened her eyes and looked around the room before settling her gaze on me. She shot straight up in her bed.

"What the hell are you doing here?" She asked.

"The nurse called me and told me what happened, so I came over to help."

She rubbed her head and looked at me wide-eyed.

"That was a pretty bad fall," I said trying to make conversation.

Tanya frowned at me and made her way across the other side of the bed away from me.

"Are you trying to kill me?" She was serious.

If I could get away with it I would.

"What? No!"

She sniffed the air near me and said,

"You don't smell like alcohol, so you might actually be telling the truth."

I wanted to take offense to that but there was no point.

"Would you like me to get you some water from the kitchen?"

I was surprised at my own act of kindness and from the weird look on Tanya's face, she was too.

"Sure, but you best believe there are cameras in the kitchen if you try anything funny," she said.

I rolled my eyes and laughed at her. She didn't realize how hard this was for me to even be in her presence like this.

Why the hell did they have cameras in their kitchen? Freaks! They probably did it on the counter and recorded themselves to watch later. *Ugh. Why couldn't that be me?*

When I entered the kitchen, I noticed the theme was apples. There were apples everywhere. Apples on the curtains, apple potholders, apple canisters, apple pictures, apple dishtowels, these chic really loves fucking apples. What caught my eye next was an untouched bottle of wine sitting on the counter near a prescription bottle of morphine. I picked up the pill bottle and noticed Tanya's name written across the top. It was practically empty. I looked at the bottle of wine. My first thought was to grab it and take a swig, but I kept seeing a vision of my dead daughter's body in my head.

"Lord, why does thou tempt me?" I said loudly. I was hoping Tanya would hear me and come distract me from wanting the alcohol.

I closed my eyes to focus. This was surely a test. I almost started shaking, because I had to pass by the bottle to get to the glasses. I reached in the cabinet and a cup fell right near where the bottle was sitting. Tightly, I gripped my hand around the neck of the bottle. My heart rate increased. I felt beads of sweat forming on my forehead. This was some bullshit. I have never experienced this before.

I touched my pocket for my cell phone, pulled it out, and quickly dialed Alice's number.

"Hi this is Alice leave a message at the sound of the beep."

Fuck!

"Alice, hi this is Portia. I am having a moment. I am touching a bottle of wine and I want to open it. Call me back."

I ended the call and grabbed the bottle twisting off the cap. I put the bottle up to my lips and was ready to take a sip until I felt my phone vibrate.

"H..hello?"

"Portia, just close your eyes and release your hand. Take a few steps backwards until you feel you are completely away from it."

It was Alice calling me back.

I did as Alice instructed. I released my grip placing the bottle back on the counter, closed my eyes, and stepped backward. There were thoughts of my little girl in my head. When I bumped into something, I looked around and saw I was standing near the fridge on the opposite side of the kitchen.

"Alice I did it I'm away from the bottle!" I was overjoyed. For the first time I felt I had conquered something.

"Good job! Remember you have control over this and you can do this. I'm at work, but I have my cell phone on me so feel free to call me at anytime," Alice said.

"Thank you Alice talk to you later," I said and pressed end on my phone.

I opened up the fridge and saw a bottle of water sitting on the shelf. I grabbed it and got away from the kitchen as fast as I could. To a normal person I would look crazy running from an inanimate object, but to a person who was struggling with drinking as much as I was this was normal. I walked back to Tanya's room to give her the water. When I returned she was sitting up on the edge of her bed putting on her shoes.

"Where are you going?" I asked.

"None of your damn business!" She said while lacing up her shoes.

I sat the bottle of water down on the night stand.

"Tanya, you shouldn't leave in your condition." I couldn't believe I was really trying to coax this girl into staying in her own house.

"What condition? I am not an alcoholic. I don't depend on alcohol to drown out my realities. I saw your ass shaking on the damn camera in the kitchen. You should have just taken a drink scaredy cat," she taunted.

That stung. No one had called me an alcoholic to my face. I wasn't going to take that.

"You are right you are not an alcoholic, I am! At least I can say what I am and get help for it instead of popping pills. I noticed your little bottle on the counter and it looks like someone is developing a habit. Most people keep that in their medicine cabinet unless they are using it on a regular basis."

Her mouth dropped open. I smiled. I won this round.

She was silent.

"You don't know me," she said through gritted teeth.

"I think I know you better than you want to believe."

We both sat staring at each other. After about two minutes she broke her stare and got up from the bed.

"I am going to check on Terrance," she said.

"I'll go with you." I started towards the door.

Tanya ran in front of me blocking my path.

"Don't bother."

"Look Tanya, this isn't easy for me to be around you no more than it is for you. At some point we will have to deal with it."

"What if I don't want to deal with it? What if I want to have Terrance's final moments to myself? I am his wife and I think I deserve that much. At least you have his son. Once he dies I don't have anything left of him, but memories," she said tearfully.

I felt bad. She was right. I would always have Terrance Jr.

"Well can I just say goodbye?" I asked.

She took a moment before she responded.

"I guess," she said and moved out of the way.

I followed her back to the room Terrance was in. The nurses were sitting nearby and making notes in a chart.

"Tanya, glad to see you doing a lot better," one of the nurses said.

It took a long moment for me to look at Terrance. He still looked the same as he did when I first arrived.

"Nurse how is he?" I asked.

The nurse gave me a sad look.

"Right now he is slightly responsive which just means he isn't brain dead yet. If you two want to talk to him that may help us determine his brain waves better."

Tanya looked at me.

"She doesn't need to say anything to him," she said referring to me.

I rolled my eyes at her and approached the right side of his bed anyway as she approached the left. I watched as she took his hand in hers.

"Terrance, its Tanya I want you to know that I have decided to move into the house with Amber and Portia as you requested," she said.

I gave her a strange look.

"Portia is here with me and we are getting along just fine," she continued.

I looked over at his monitor sure that it was going to go off or blow up at the sound of Tanya's lies.

"You know he can hear you right?" I asked.

Tanya cut her eyes at me before whispering to me,

"Are you going to work with me on trying to keep him alive or work against me?"

I sighed loud enough for a dead person buried six feet underneath the ground to hear. I inhaled before grabbing his hand into mine, a gesture I had never done unless there was sex involved.

"Terrance, this is Portia and I need you to survive, so you can be there for our son TJ. He needs you. We need you."

Tanya looked at me like she wanted to punch me in the mouth. I didn't care I was telling the truth. I did need Terrance. He still owed me back child support.

His brain monitor moved rapidly.

"Wow, either he can hear you, or he dislikes you very much," the nurse said.

This time Tanya and I both cut our eyes at her.

"I'm sorry I didn't mean to be rude," she said and continued writing on his chart.

We continued stroking his hand and talking to him for the next twenty minutes, until I was sure the lies we were feeding him would guarantee us a seat in hell. Once we were done we both walked out of the room into the living room. I was curious to know if Tanya was only talking when she said she was moving in to the house with Amber and me.

"Were you just saying that to make Terrance respond, or are you really going to move into the house?" I asked.

Tanya looked at me. Her shoulders dropped in defeat.

"I am really going to move in. I been fighting him for so long on every single thing I feel the least I could do is fulfill his last dying wish. Terrance and I have been through so much together. Babies, you, Amber, his sickness, it's been one hell of a ride. I'm tired of fighting!"

When she stopped talking there were tears in her eyes. At this point I didn't know whether to walk away or wait. I was never good at the friendship thing. I went with my gut instinct and touched her hand sure that she would punch me or move her hand away from mine. Instead, she grasped my hand tighter as the tears fell down her cheeks. We just sat there in the hallway silent. This was a moment I don't think either one of us would forget.

Amber

I walked in to the house setting my keys on the counter as if I was floating on a cloud. Tanya had called me earlier to tell me the news of Terrance being put on life support. My heart was broken. In some way I guess I did still love Terrance. I had his firstborn son and memories I was holding on to from when we were younger. It didn't help seeing my son's face to remind me of his father every day.

I stepped outside to grab the mail from the mailbox. The sun was out and the weather was beginning to warm up. Chicago's spring is always colder than others so summer is always a welcomed season when it arrives.

Considering all the things that have happened over the past few months I was ready for some warm weather.

I sifted through the mail trying to separate my mail from Portia's until I came across a letter addressed to Portia, Tanya and I.

I figured since my name was on it I could open it and pass it to them when I was done reading it.

I pulled out the stationery and read the letter.

I can't believe I am writing this letter, but it needs to be done. I know this information isn't coming at the right time, but then I had to think exactly what the right time is. I thought you should know that there is some very important information you need to know. Please meet up with me at the Starbucks downtown on Michigan Street tomorrow at 8p.m. I will tell you everything.

Mariah G.

I closed the letter. Who in the hell was Mariah G.? What did she have to tell us about this house? I called Rebecca immediately.

"Is there a return address on it?" She asked.

I looked at the envelope.

"No."

"What city or state was it mailed from?"

"Florida," I told her.

"It might be a scam. I'd be careful. You just came into a large amount of money and now you are getting a weird letter from some random female telling you to meet her? Sounds fishy if you ask me," Rebecca said.

"Yea, but what if it's not a sham? What if Terrance is hiding something from us?" I was convinced there was more to it than a scam.

"I highly doubt that."

We were both silent. Rebecca started speaking.

"Amber, please don't go acting like a white girl trying to find out who this person is. You know in those scary movies those types of women always die first," Rebecca laughed at her statement.

"Shut up this is no scary movie this is real life. I am curious to know what this woman knows. If it has anything to do with this house I want to know, especially seeing as how this is my home now," I replied.

I heard Portia close the downstairs door. "I'll call you back later," I told Rebecca.

"Amber, please don't do anything stupid. Call me back."

I hung up the phone and walked out of my room and down the long hallway towards the spiral staircase. Portia was dragging a suitcase up the stairs while Tanya was bringing in two black suitcases.

"Hey Portia, hey Tanya how are you doing?" I asked.

Tanya stopped and gave me a very concerned look.

"The question is how are *you*? I heard what happened are you okay?" She asked.

I was embarrassed. It was all over the news about me getting shot by my mom.

"I'm okay. I still have some minor pain, but for the most part I am just glad to be out of that hospital."

I looked Tanya over. She looked worn out and a lot thinner. She gave me a weak smile before setting her bag down in the foyer.

"When you two have a minute I have a letter that was sent to us that you need to read," I told them.

"It's probably about the insurance money disbursement," Tanya said.

I shook my head.

"No this letter is weird. It was sent from a Mariah G. from Florida. She said she wants to meet up with us tomorrow night which is actually tonight at Starbucks."

"Mariah G? Could that be Mariah Gonzales?" Portia asked.

Tanya and I both looked at Portia confused.

"Okay what's going on? Who is Mariah Gonzales and why the hell does she want to meet with us?" Tanya asked.

"I would think you being the wife you would have more information about this house than we do, "Portia responded.

"Now hold on you both know Terrance made this decision alone. I learned about this house and this *arrangement* the same way you did and you know that," Tanya said.

I passed her the letter. After reading it she said,

"I never heard of her. I guess we should meet her to find out what she has to say."

Portia started rummaging through her purse.

"Where is my pistol at?" She asked us like we knew.

"Don't be stupid remember you are still on probation," Tanya said.

I was impressed with how they seemed to be getting along.

"True, but if she is on some mess I will be prepared. Wait, now that I think back Mariah Gonzales was at this house when I came to see it before...." Portia stopped midsentence. "Before Teyah and TJ were injured."

"What? Why was she here? What did she say?" Tanya asked.

"She actually showed me the house and said she and her husband own it."

"Well we should go find out what's going on. I'll drive," Tanya said grabbing her keys.

We followed her out to her BMW. This situation was getting better and better.

Tanya

We arrived at Starbucks and found Mariah Gonzales sitting by the window. She was dressed like money, big money, wearing a very expensive pink, silk, pashmina scarf around her neck. Her long, wavy black hair was perfectly coiffed. She looked like she belonged in someone's magazine. She stood up to greet us.

"Thank you for coming. I wasn't sure if anybody would receive the letter so I addressed it to all three of you," she sat back down.

I took a seat near the window while Portia and Amber sat down next to each other.

"What is this about?" I asked her.

She pulled a document out of her Pink Hermes Birkin bag.

"You have a Birkin? Oh my God I love your purse," Portia said.

She was drooling over it like a kid in a candy store.

Mariah smiled.

"Do you want it? I have another one in a different color," she motioned towards the bag.

"Get the fuck out of here you have got to be kidding me?" Portia screamed.

Amber and I watched as Mariah emptied the contents out of the bag and passed it right to Portia.

"It must be a knockoff," Amber whispered to me.

I nodded my head in agreement. There was no way any woman in her right mind would just give away a $20,000 purse to someone she barely knew. I was in amazement as Portia sniffed the purse and searched the inside like a detective.

"It's real!" She said.

Mariah laughed.

"Of course it's real now let's get down to business. The house you currently occupy has been put up for a short sale. I have accepted an offer and I'm willing to give you thirty days to vacate the premises."

All three of our mouths dropped open.

"What do you mean a short sale?" Amber asked.

"My husband bought this house for us to live in!" I said a little too loud. Some of the patrons in Starbucks turned around at the tone of my voice.

"Why would you let us move in if the house wasn't paid for?" Portia said more to me than Mariah.

Mariah frowned.

"We gave Terrance the opportunity to try it out before buying. I thought by letting you guys get a feel for the home it would convince him to complete the sale. He never signed the final paperwork and since we were anxious to sell we put the offer back out there and someone accepted," she responded.

There was silence at the table.

"Tanya, don't you have power of attorney? Can't you do something?" Amber asked me.

She and Portia looked at me for an answer.

"I do, but it won't make a bit of difference if she has already accepted another offer. Is the offer still negotiable?" I turned my attention to Mariah.

She looked impatient.

"I'm sorry I held off as long as I could."

"Did you know Terrance has a terminal illness? Doesn't that count for anything? He has stage four-lung cancer and is now on life support. There was no way he could have signed anything, because he hasn't been healthy enough to do so."

I was trying to plead the case on my husband's behalf.

"Cancer, wow I'm so sorry to hear that! I just seen Terrance a few months ago and he looked just fine. I guess things can change in a matter of seconds," Mariah said.

"Yes it can. For the past couple of months Terrance has been in a hospital bed with round the clock nurses suffering from a collapsed lung. The only time he left the house was to attend his daughter's…. funeral and that was a month ago. Now he is on life support so it can be any moment now," I said while looking at Portia. She was staring out the window with a sad look on her face at the mention of her daughter.

"I knew it had to be something when he failed to show up for our final meeting to sign the paper work. I called and called but received no answers. I even sent letters to his attorney Jason Ellis. My final letter was the one you all received."

"Jason Ellis? He isn't Terrance's attorney. He isn't even practicing law for that matter," I advised her.

We all looked at each other puzzled on how Jason was involved in this.

Mariah frowned before speaking.

"I don't understand. I have been communicating with a Jason Ellis who said he is Terrance's attorney. He has met with me on several occasions and is the one who informed Terrance of the house I had for sale."

"Tanya, were you aware of this?" Portia asked.

"No, this is news to me. Terrance told me that Rebecca Smith was acting as his attorney," I said.

"Is this some type of joke?" Portia asked Mariah.

"Please let me reassure you I am not here on any games, nor would I make anything up," she said defensively.

"I don't understand this. Something doesn't sound right. Mariah can I have a phone number to reach you at? I need to get to the bottom of this." I said.

She passed me her card with her contact information on it.

I stood up to leave and the other women followed my lead.

"It was nice meeting you. I am sure we will be in touch. I will have my real attorney draw up a cease and desist letter advising you not to proceed with the short sale." I proceeded to walk away.

"I would advise you not to challenge me on this house," Mariah stated.

I stopped and turned around.

"Sweetie, you aren't the only wife with a husband who has a few dollars to throw around. I am challenging you and I am advising you that you don't want to take me on. I have big money too," I said.

Mariah gave me a smug look before shaking her head.

"Touché my dear we shall see how this goes," she said.

Portia ran up and stopped Mariah from saying anything else.

"Thanks for the bag I'm going to hurry up and leave before you try to take it back," Portia said and ran by me.

Amber had a very confused look on her face. We both were in a state of confusion, but I was more than determined to find out what the hell was going on.

Portia

We all rode in Tanya's car in silence. Terrance had lied to us in some way I was sure of it. Now we were all about to be homeless. I clutched my new bag to my chest. I wanted a drink so bad. This sobriety shit was fucking me up.

"Portia are you alright?"

Amber looked at me with concern. I was shaking and rocking back and forth.

"She probably wants a drink," Tanya said while glaring at me through her rearview mirror.

"You know what Tanya you need to just drive your car and leave me the fuck alone," I said.

"No alchy you need to get a hold of yourself. We are all going through this situation together."

I hit her in the back of her head with my bag without even thinking.

The car came to an abrupt stop causing us all to jerk forward. Tanya rubbed the back of her head and then turned around, grabbed the bag and slapped me in the face with it.

"I am tired of being nice. This shit isn't going to work between you and me. If you so much as lay a hand on me again we will be planning two funerals," Tanya said.

Amber had her hand over her mouth to keep from laughing. I opened the door to get out just as a car sped by and almost ran into me. I had to slam the door to move out the way.

"Don't be slamming my door like that," Tanya yelled.

"Did you see me almost get hit?" I asked.

"Come on Portia, get back in the car we have bigger issues to work out than you throwing a tantrum right now," Amber chimed in.

"Amber, shut the hell up. If Tanya hit you I don't think you'd be sitting there either."

I heard Amber say to Tanya in what was supposed to be a whisper,

"She's right if you would have hit me I would be standing outside too."

"She hit me first," Tanya replied.

"Tanya, you sound like one of the kids," Amber said.

It was quiet and I assumed Tanya was either pouting or waiting on me to get in. I sighed loud enough so she could hear and just as I was opening the door, I heard the sound of squealing tires.

The car I had dodged earlier came barreling towards me at full speed.

"Portia get out of the way!" Tanya screamed.

I slammed the door again and hopped on top of Tanya's BMW as the car side swiped the driver's side. I fell on the other side near the sidewalk.

Tanya and Amber screamed and jumped out the car through the passenger side door, and ran around to where I was lying on the sidewalk.

"What the hell was that? You would think someone was trying to kill us," Tanya screamed. "Look at my car!"

"Did anyone get a look at the license plate number?" Amber asked.

I was too shaken to respond. Tanya was accessing the damage to her car. Once she was done we all got back inside.

"I think that car is following us," Tanya said nervously

I turned around looking out the back window and noticed the same car trailing behind us.

"Oh my God that's the car," I said.

"I'm gonna take the I-90 and see if I can lose them in traffic."

Tanya floored her BMW towards the ramp to the expressway until we were doing 80 mph in the traffic. I watched as she darted in and out of traffic flawlessly, trying to lose the person following behind us.

"They are still on our tail," Amber said. She too had turned around to look out the back window.

"I can't believe this is happening," Tanya said still whipping the car in and around traffic.

"I can't believe you are driving this car like you have been chased before," I said.

Tanya continued jumping from lane to lane until we were sure the car was no longer able to follow us.

"I think I lost them," she said as she cut a sharp right in front of a truck and exited the freeway. She turned down a side street, made two lefts in an alley, and a right until we were back in local traffic.

When we arrived back at the house we saw someone run from the back yard, hop the fence, and dash down the street.

"Did ya'll just see that?" Tanya asked.

"Yes," Amber and I replied in unison.

"Do you think someone was trying to break in?" Amber asked.

"No, it was the welcoming committee welcoming us to the neighborhood. What else could it be?" I said.

Amber rolled her eyes at me. Tanya parked the car in the driveway and I pulled my pistol out of my purse.

"Why the hell do you always have a gun?" Tanya asked.

"Conceal and carry boo. I grew up in the hood that's why and I really think someone is trying to kill us," I replied.

Tanya just shook her head and said to Amber,

"Let's stay close to Cleo here, so she can shoot anyone who gets close to us and go to jail for it."

"Tanya, you are not funny," I moved away from her, took the safety off the gun, and closed the car door quietly.

"Who's Cleo?" Amber whispered.

"Haven't you ever watched the movie *Set It Off*? The character Queen Latifah played was named Cleo," I told her.

"I don't think I have ever seen that movie," Amber responded.

"What, you only date black men, but you don't watch black movies?"

"Portia, don't start with me!"

Before I could think of another good come back, I noticed a wallet on the ground near the door. I picked it up. Inside, there was a condom and a ticket to a strip club.

"Surely whoever just ran off is a man. A sloppy man at that there is a phone number inside."

I handed the wallet over to Tanya for further inspection while I looked around the side of the house.

"You have got to be kidding me," she screamed. "This is Terrance's old cell phone number on the back of this card! Quick, give me your cell phone so I can call it."

I handed her my phone.

"I'm going to put it on speaker so we can all hear who picks up," Tanya said.

She dialed the number. Someone picked up on the first ring.

A manly voice said, "Is it done?"

"Is what done muthafucka? Are you the one that just tried to kill us?" I shouted.

The line went dead.

"Damn it Portia, you just ruined our chance to find out who that was," Tanya said frustrated.

"If you ask me it sounded like Terrance."

We both looked at Amber.

"How could that be if he is on life support?" I asked looking at her for an answer.

"Maybe he woke up," she said convincingly.

"Amber, do you know something we don't?" Tanya asked.

"No, I was just saying. I think we should call the police before going inside."

"Technically, we aren't supposed to be living here according to Mariah Gonzales, so I'm going to take my chances," Tanya said.

"I have a gun so I'm good."

We unlocked the door to the house and each took turns opening doors and closets and turning on lights. By the time we had covered the entire house we were pretty sure no one was there. My room was suddenly too big for me, so I grabbed the comforter off my bed and went downstairs to what was known as the family room. There was a plush, red reclining sectional sofa and a projector screen for the TV. Tanya apparently had the same idea since I found her curled up on one end of the couch with her pink comforter. Amber came downstairs minutes later with her comforter and pillow.

"Aww look, it's a baby mama slumber party," Amber said taking the middle of the couch.

"Amber, please shut up before I go back upstairs and get my gun and wait for you to fall asleep," I told her.

"I really think you need to look into anger management classes," she suggested.

"Whatever, this situation is really crazy. I almost got hit, we been chased by some unknown car, and I have absolutely no place to stay. Tanya, at least you still have the condo to go back to, and Amber you have your parents' house."

"Did you forget my mother shot me? I am not moving back in with her, so we are in the same position. I'll just have to find a two bedroom apartment somewhere for Nathan and I to go to." An expression crossed Amber's face that I couldn't read.

I noticed Tanya was in deep thought.

"Did either one of you receive any money yet?" She asked.

"I know I didn't. I signed the forms and sent them to the attorney as requested, but I checked my account and it was the same balance I had before," I told her.

Amber was quiet.

"What about you Amber?" Tanya asked.

"No," she replied quietly.

"That's weird weren't you the first to move into the house?" Tanya questioned.

"Yes."

"So, you should have received some money right after you moved in," Tanya stated.

I watched Amber as she thought about a reply. She was quiet for awhile.

"I mean it was no big deal a few dollars nothing major like was promised. I figured it was my child support payment."

My mouth dropped open.

"Bitch, you getting child support? Oh that's fucked up. Terrance is paying the white girl, but he isn't paying me."

I stood up.

"Portia, calm down you know why he stopped paying you. You were taking the money to go out and drink on his dime, and we had to pay for supplies for your beauty salon, plus we had to cover the damages to the shop that burnt down remember? Now sit back down." Tanya patted the couch.

I continued to stand.

"That doesn't excuse him from paying for his kids."

"Correction, don't you mean his kid? You know damn well Terrance took very good care of you and your children." Tanya gave me a look that I wanted to slap off of her face.

Before I could say something to her about her comment my cell phone started ringing. It was the number we had dialed earlier. I showed Tanya the number and she pushed the button to answer it. Before she could say anything the person hung up and Amber left the room. Some weird shit was going on and I was beginning to think Amber had something to do with it.

Amber

My palms were sweating as I paced my bedroom floor back and forth. I should have told them how much money I received from Terrance, but I kept that to myself in case I needed to get away. This situation was getting weird. I just knew that voice on the phone was Terrance. It sounded just like him. I started packing my bags. There was no way I was about to stay in this house any longer and wait for more things to happen. I called the automated teller at my bank to recheck my balance.

"Your current balance is $32.96. You have no pending deposits at this time."

I screamed.

Portia came running into my room with that stupid gun in her hand.

"What's wrong? What happened?"

Tanya appeared seconds later.

"What? What's going on?"

I had to tell them.

"My account balance is only $32.96."

"Bitch, are you serious? You had me sprint up all the stairs and down this damn hallway because your account balance is low? I should hit you in your head," Portia said.

Tanya frowned at me. I took a deep breath before speaking.

"I didn't tell you guys that when I first moved in here Terrance deposited $500,000 into my account. I verified it at the bank and it was there. My friend Rebecca and I spent some of it. Now it's gone."

"You had half a million dollars in your account?" Tanya asked.

"See I told you she was holding out," Portia said.

"Terrance promised you half a million dollars?"

Tanya was acting like she had no idea. I thought he promised the same amount to everyone. Of course with her being the wife she would get more.

"I assumed that's what Portia and I were getting."

"Well I didn't get anything."

Portia sounded like a child.

Tanya shook her head repeatedly.

"He never told me what the starting amount would be."

"Sounds like you don't know your husband as much as you think you do," Portia responded.

I gave her a look. She always said whatever came to her mind no matter whose feelings were hurt in the process.

"Before anything else gets started let's just get some sleep. It's been a long day for all of us," I suggested.

Portia gave me a funny look while looking at my suitcase near the door.

"Where were you getting ready to run to Amber?"

"What? I wasn't going anywhere."

"Yea, right I have reason to think you are in on whatever scam Terrance is pulling," Portia said accusingly.

"I swear to you I'm not. I was going to go stay in a hotel just in case something else happened. I have never been around drama like this before!"

Tanya and Portia started laughing.

"Are you serious right now? Remember your mother just shot you over your black boyfriend? If that isn't drama for your ass I don't know what else is," Portia said.

She had a point.

"Why don't we all go stay at a hotel. Whoever was at this house earlier and chasing us in the street might come back looking to do us harm or worse," Tanya said.

"Who is going to pay for the room? I'm broke and from the look of it so is Amber."

We were silent waiting on Tanya to say she would cover the room.

"I guess I'll cover the room."

"Do you think we should take my car since we were already · chased down in yours?" I asked Tanya.

"White girl has a point," Portia said.

I shot her a look.

"Maybe we should take our own cars," Tanya said.

"No Tanya I think to be safe we should stay together. We separate and who knows what can happen," I said.

She threw her hands up in surrender and we headed to my car.

The ride was quiet as we were all deep in thought.

The more I thought about it things weren't adding up and Terrance was the only one who had answers. I wanted to see where Tanya's head was so I asked her a question.

"Tanya, did it ever occur to you that Terrance could be setting us all up for a fail?"

Tanya was quiet before she responded.

"I have wanted to pretend that he would never do that, but after all the things we have been through tonight and the past couple of months, anything is possible," she said.

Portia chimed in,

"If he is setting us up there will be hell to pay. I have practically lost my son, almost got ran over and now I have no money. I say let's go to your house and shake that muthafucka awake and demand some answers."

"How in the hell do you propose we do that? You can't shake someone awake who is on life support," Tanya said.

"Well this will be a day in history because I am going to damn sure try. Come on Amber turn this car around and head to Tanya's house."

I waited for Tanya's response. When she waved her hands in the air I turned the car around and headed back to her condo. Once we arrived she directed me to park my car in her parking spot in the underground parking lot. She used her electronic key to activate the elevator. The wait was making me anxious. When we reached their floor a chill swept over my body. Something wasn't right. I could feel it.

"Wait a second ya'll something isn't right," I said.

"Damn sure it isn't," Portia said.

Tanya looked at me before continuing down the hall to her door. It was already opened. Gently she pushed it opened all the way and we went in together. It was so quiet you could hear a pin drop. The sound of the clock ticking was the only thing that could be heard. We followed Tanya as she made her way through the condo. We stopped outside of what look like a den. The doors were closed. Tanya turned the knob gently and opened the door. I could feel Portia breathing on my neck that's how close we were.

"You have got to be kidding me," Tanya said.

I was afraid to go through the door. I stood right where I was and let Portia go around me.

"Where the fuck is Terrance at?" I heard Tanya ask.

"I'm sorry he's dead. They just took him off of life support two hours ago," the woman replied.

My heart sank at the sound of her voice. What in the hell was she doing here? I had to get answers. I entered the room and looked Rebecca in the eyes.

"What the hell are you doing here Rebecca?" I asked.

"Wait, weren't you the bitch at the house when I moved in?" Portia asked.

"You know this woman?" Tanya asked me.

"Yes this is Rebecca Smith. She's my attorney and best friend."

"How in the hell did you get in my house?" Tanya asked.

Rebecca shook her head.

"You women are all pathetic. You all had access to a good man with lots of money and somehow, someway you all found a way to fuck that up."

"You didn't answer my question. How the hell did you get in my house and what the hell are you doing here?" Tanya demanded.

"I came to collect what's mine," Rebecca said patting a black duffle bag.

"What the hell are you talking about Becky?"

I asked her thoroughly confused.

"Amber, you were always so ignorant and naive. All of you for that matter," she said pointing to Tanya and Portia.

"Who in the hell are you calling ignorant?"

Portia moved near Rebecca.

I watched Tanya pull out her cell phone.

"Jason and I have been seeing each other for years now. He told me all about this arrangement Terrance came up with and I told him it was a good idea. Matter of fact I'm the one who printed up the agreement for him and told Terrance I would represent him. I suggested he look into purchasing the house from Mariah Gonzalez. She and I went to school together," Rebecca smiled an evil smile.

I watched her mouth move, but my brain was cloudy. I finally put it all together.

"So it was you! That was your mother's car that came flying at us earlier and almost hit Portia! You are the buyer that just bought the house from Mariah aren't you? How could you do this? I trusted you!"

Rebecca laughed.

"Amber, you trust everybody. If you weren't so naïve you would learn to look into things on your own instead of calling me all the damn time. Now you won't have to worry about me anymore."

I looked at both Tanya and Portia. Tanya's mouth was open and Portia looked ready to fight.

"You are my attorney for goodness sake! I called you to get legal advice and because I considered you my friend. I thought you would have my best interest at heart!"

The tears stung my eyes. I was hurt. First Terrance, my mother, now my best friend this was unbelievable.

"Fuck all this emotional shit. Someone needs to beat her ass," Portia said.

Tanya had to hold Portia back.

"You still haven't told us how you got in the house," Tanya said.

"Does it matter?" Rebecca replied.

"Yes it does matter. Where is Terrance? Why didn't they call me if he was pulled off the machine?"

Rebecca looked suspiciously towards the closet door. She was hiding something. Portia was clutching the side of her waist very tight. I knew she had brought that pistol with her. Tanya followed my gaze.

"Rebecca, tell the truth do you know where Terrance is?" I asked.

"I told you he is dead. They took him off the machine," she said.

"You are lying. I know when you are lying. I have been around you for too long."

Rebecca was getting nervous, but I was the only one who knew that. She shifted her weight.

Tanya was watching me closely for any signs that I knew something. I directed my eyes towards the closet since Rebecca kept look over there. Whatever she was hiding was in that closet. All four of us stood there in silence. An idea struck me. I walked over to Portia and asked her for her cell phone. She handed it to me and I pressed the number we had dialed earlier that Tanya said was Terrance's old cell phone. I heard the sound of the phone ringing coming from the closet.

"Excuse me I need to make a call," Rebecca told us.

"You just stay right there. Portia make sure she doesn't move," I instructed.

Portia happily pulled out her pistol.

"I have been waiting to use this thing all day."

Portia walked over to Rebecca and hit her upside the head with the end of the gun. She fell to the ground.

"Was that really necessary? I said make sure she doesn't move."

"That's what I did she won't be moving for awhile with that gash in her head!" Portia replied.

Tanya and I both walked over to the closet. I grabbed a vase on a nearby table and held it up as Tanya slowly opened the door. I screamed. What tumbled out of the closet was unbelievable.

Tanya

This was the sickest thing I had ever seen in my life. When I opened up the closet door the bodies of the two nurses tumbled out. The three of us screamed. They had been beaten to death and then gagged. Before I knew what I was doing I grabbed the pistol out of Portia's hands and pointed it at Rebecca's head.

"Please don't! It's not what it looks like," Rebecca screamed.

I ignored her.

"Where is Terrance?"

I pointed the gun at her head. I wasn't sure how to use a gun, but I watched enough TV to fake like I did.

I looked back at Portia and Amber. Amber looked sick. Portia was feigning for a drink I could see it in her eyes.

"Tanya, please I had nothing to do with this! You have to believe me," Rebecca cried.

"Are they dead?" Portia asked.

"It looks like it," Amber said.

I nudged both nurses with my foot and neither one of them moved. It was eerie.

"What kind of sick asshole would kill a damn nurse?" I asked.

"I don't understand. Rebecca, where is Terrance?" Amber asked.

"I told you it's not what it looks like, and I had nothing to do with this!" She said.

Portia was unusually quiet.

My hand started shaking as I continued pointing the gun at Rebecca's head.

"Just put the gun down Tanya and we can talk about this," Rebecca said trying to coax me out of shooting her.

"You ruined our lives!" Amber screamed out.

"You ruined your own lives. Terrance found three of the dumbest women and played each one of you in his game," Rebecca responded.

My finger was on the trigger of the pistol and I wanted so desperately to put a bullet through this woman's body, but I am not a killer. I have never killed anyone in my life. Rebecca was too calm for me.

This situation made no sense. I was watching Portia trying to ease her way out of the room.

"Portia!" I called her name.

"I can't handle this too many bodies, too much death. I need a drink!"

I thought about the bottle of wine that was in my kitchen and knew that's where she would be headed.

"Amber, stop her please she is going for my liquor cabinet in the kitchen."

Amber ran out the room after her.

When I turned around Rebecca was standing in front of me and before I could react she was trying to wrestle the gun out of my hand. She wasn't any bigger than I was, but her strength was comparable to two men. We struggled back and forth until the gun went off.

Portia

I made it to the kitchen in a matter of seconds and grabbed the bottle of wine that was sitting there on the kitchen counter. I opened the top and was getting ready to pour the liquid down my throat when Amber came running into the kitchen.

"Portia stop! Don't do it! You been sober for awhile now don't go back."

"Amber, leave me alone. No one knows what's best for me."

I put the bottle up to my lips and closed my eyes. Amber came and smacked the bottle out of my hands which made a deafening pop sound, but then I realized that was not the sound of the bottle hitting the floor. That was a gunshot. We both looked at each other fearing the worst. I didn't think I could take looking at any more bodies. Seeing Teyah in her casket and then those two nurses lying still on that floor was enough. Amber walked out of the kitchen and I followed closely behind her. We approached the room slowly afraid of what we were going to find.

When we walked into the room Tanya had a look of bewilderment on her face. When I saw who was standing near her it was clear as to why.

"Jason, what the fuck how, what,...?" I walked over to him to touch him just to be sure I was not dreaming.

He was holding my pistol in his hand. I couldn't even guess how he had got a hold of it. I looked over at Rebecca bleeding from her side. Amber shook her head repeatedly.

"Okay you know with all this noise someone had to have called the police and I'm on probation and not trying to go back to jail," I said.

I had to find my way out of this situation.

"All of you can go. I'll handle this right here," Jason said.

He didn't have to tell me twice. I gathered my belongings.

"What are you doing?" Amber asked me.

"What does it look like? I'm not getting locked up for none of you fools. I don't know about you but jail is not where I want to be."

I proceeded to leave out of the room until Amber grabbed my arm.

"We can't leave Tanya to deal with this alone," she said.

"Well *we* don't have to, but *I* am."

"It's not right," she pulled me out of earshot. "Something isn't right about this. Have you noticed that Jason always seems to be front and center of all the drama? Think about it. He was at the hospital, Teyah's funeral, and now this. Rebecca said she didn't have anything to do with this part of it. My gut is telling me he has something to do with this entire thing not to mention no one seems to know where the hell Terrance is."

"And my gut is telling me to get the fuck out of here before the police arrest my black ass."

I wasn't trying to play captain save a hoe at this time.

"Come on Portia, this isn't right and you know it. The three of us should stick together, because we are the ones who got played," Amber pleaded.

"Bitch, I'm not trying to go to jail! I hear what you saying, but do you hear me? Grab Tanya's ass and tell her to come on. I'll be outside in the car."

I could hear the sirens outside. I made my way down the hall to the stairwell. I was glad I had on my tennis shoes. I skipped two stairs at a time until I reached the garage. I pushed the door open and wouldn't you know who was standing there when I opened the door, the police.

Damn!

Amber

I watched Portia run down the hallway to the stairwell. I wanted to run right behind her, but I was truly stuck. I walked back into the condo to get Tanya. When I walked back into the room she was holding on to one of the nurse's hand.

"Tanya, I hear the police outside and I'm sure they are on their way up."

"I know. I called them earlier. I can't leave them laying here like this. They been taking care of Terrance all this time and this is how they are repaid? This isn't right," she said.

I looked around the room for Jason and Rebecca.

"Where did they go?"

Tanya shrugged her shoulders. They only had one exit and I didn't see either one of them when I came back in the door.

I didn't trust their disappearance. That could only mean they were trying to escape, or planning to do more damage. I walked around the condo looking for both of them. I heard voices when I approached Tanya's bedroom.

"I can't believe you shot me. I told you this shit wasn't going to work. Then you let that ghetto bitch hit me in my head with her damn gun," I heard Rebecca say.

"It's only a flesh wound stop crying about it. I didn't know what else to do. They weren't even supposed to be here. If you would have done what you were supposed to we wouldn't be going through this right now," Jason said.

"What are you talking about? I tried to run them off the road as planned and I sent my cousin to the house just like you asked. I don't know what happened."

"What happened is you should have taken care of Amber first when you stayed at the damn house with her. One by one they would have all fallen." I heard Jason get quiet.

I pinned myself to the wall.

"Did you transfer all of the money over?" He asked.

"Yes baby I did."

Baby?

I heard what sounded like a kiss.

"Good, let's get out of here the police are downstairs so we have to go out a different way. There is a fire escape right outside of the second bedroom," said Jason.

This was ridiculous. I listened as both of them moved around the room. I tiptoed to the kitchen grabbing whatever knife I could find. There was no way I was going to let them just walk away from this mess. I walked in the room just as Jason was making his way out of the window. There were no signs of Rebecca so I assumed she was on the fire escape already.

"Just where do you think you are going?" I asked him.

Jason looked at me.

"Don't try to be a savior now Amber."

"I can't believe you Jason! Terrance is your best friend!"

"Was, he was my best friend. Don't act all high and mighty as if you have never done wrong in your lifetime."

"I have never tried to kill anyone over several million dollars."

"Who said I killed anyone?"

Rebecca stuck her head back in the window.

"Jason come on we don't have time to talk to her."

I wanted to walk right up and stab Rebecca in her heart since that is what she was doing to me. I saw Rebecca's eyes widen.

The sound of the police officer standing behind me caused me to jump.

"Put the weapon down and put your hands over your head," the officer yelled loudly in my ear.

"I didn't do anything it's them you want," I pointed towards the window.

"Do what I asked you to do now!" The cop screamed again.

I dropped the butcher knife I was holding, and put my hands over my head. The officer forced me to my knees as he handcuffed me. I sat helplessly watching as Jason and Rebecca continued down the fire escape. Two other officers ran to the window. I was sure they had gotten away, but then I remembered we were nine stories up.

"Put the gun down!"

I wasn't sure who the officer was talking to, but when they both pulled out their guns I knew the ending was going to be ugly. I could vaguely hear Rebecca's voice.

"I'm not going to jail for anyone."

"Becky, listen don't do this. Put the gun down and we can talk this over." It sounded like the cop knew her.

This was truly unbelievable. Rebecca had done a complete 360'.

How do you go from being a respected attorney to a money hungry gun toting bitch?

The officer escorted me into the hallway of Tanya's condo and I heard shots fired. I knew either she or Jason had been shot. I wasn't sure why I was being arrested, but I was sure this would be my first and last time. I made a vow that as soon as this mess was over I was going to take my son and separate myself from all this drama as soon as possible.

Jason

Damn!

The cops shot me at close range right in the chest, so I knew I didn't have a shot on surviving. Rebecca pulled out the damn gun and pointed it right at the officer's face. Screaming and crying about how she isn't going to jail. *Dumb ass bitch!* I tried to knock it out of her hand, but from their viewpoint it looked like I was trying to take it from her and shoot at them.

I should have killed all these bitches myself. Terrance was lucky he was dying already. Rebecca was going to be my cover until I could get my hands on the rest of the money and then I was going to let her go. I watched as she slid down the fire escape while the officers fired at her. I thought back to the conversation she and I had months ago.

****

"You know Terrance is a multi millionaire right? He just got the settlement money from his case with his job," Rebecca said to me.

"How do you know?" I asked.

"I was the attorney working the case."

"So what are you telling me for?"

"He is trying to set up some arrangement for Tanya and his kids' mothers to get the money if they agree to move into one house together."

I laughed.

"All three of them, Portia included? That shit will never work," I said.

Rebecca laughed.

"I know I tried to tell him that, but he thinks after he coaxes all of them into it they will agree. I know my girl Amber is naïve, so she will be the first to bite, but those other two I don't know."

"Tanya is not going to accept being under the same roof with Portia. It's enough she has a child by him. What does all of this have to do with me?"

Rebecca cleared her throat.

"You are the next closest thing to him besides Tanya. He is going to die anyway from the lung cancer. I say we devise a plan to get the money away from him and we skip town so we can be together."

Rebecca was truly dick whipped. I had met up with her on a number of occasions at her office and it didn't take me long to get her panties on the floor.

"Nah, he is my best friend I can't steal his money," I told her.

"Why not, he won't be able to use it! He'll be six feet under and those three women will be living high off the hog and they don't even deserve to."

"They have his children, Rebecca!"

"So did I, but do you think his ass cared?" She said emotionally.

"What?"

253

"Terrance and I had got together in high school right before he slept with Amber's dumb ass. I got pregnant and he made me get an abortion. What pissed me off is that he ended up impregnating her and she got to keep her child."

"That was like thirteen years ago you still holding on to that shit?" I asked.

"I can't have any kids now! The abortion I had ripped my uterus and I had to have a hysterectomy."

We were silent before she started talking again.

"I want a piece of his pie and since no one knows he and I had ever slept together I plan on hitting him where it hurts just like he did me. He didn't even see how I was doing he just kept right on living his life like nothing ever happened," she said.

"Ya'll were only teenagers. His mind was immature and he might not have known how to handle a situation like that. I know I wouldn't. I just thought about something if we do this what about Amber. Isn't she your best friend?"

"Fuck her she came from a wealthy family and has always had an easy life. Now she gets a beautiful healthy child and money to go with it. I had to strip my way through school and pay for my own college tuition. My mother didn't have enough money to send me to school by herself. I chose to be a lawyer just like my father who was killed as an innocent bystander in a gas station robbery. When I passed the bar I just knew Terrance would be happy that I had something going for myself and he would get back with me. "

She was quiet for a long time and I was sure I heard her sniffling which let me know she was crying. I wasn't sure if I wanted to go through with her scheme. It would mean jeopardizing a lifelong friendship. I thought about my own life. I had no children of my own, but I did have a lot of money issues.

"Okay so if I agree to do this what do I have to do?" I asked her.

She laid down everything precisely to me and like a dumb ass I agreed to go along with it.

I just didn't know my life would be the price I would pay in the end for agreeing to something as foolish as this. I guess you live and you learn and in my case there is no more time to live. I wish I had told them the secret I was now going to die with.

Tanya

I moved myself away from the nurse's side long enough to catch what was unfolding in my bedroom. The police had Amber in the hallway in handcuffs and Jason had been shot. They were all trying to subdue Rebecca, but from the look of it she had jumped from the fire escape and tried to run. When I heard them call for an ambulance I knew someone didn't make it.

I explained the situation to the officer the best way I could, and he let me know they had Portia outside in a squad car. I knew she was on probation and this fiasco would end up sending her to jail. I had to vouch for her freedom so they wouldn't take her away. Never thought it would be me of all people trying to convince the police not to arrest her.

They ended up releasing Amber with a warning. The coroner's office was on its way to come and discard the bodies of the nurses. I was sick knowing I gave my body to Jason and all he was after was money.

No one could find Terrance. We weren't sure where they hid his body or what had happened to him.

When I looked over at Amber she had tears in her eyes as she watched the ambulance from the window.

"I truly thought she was my friend. It's sad what some people will do for money," she sobbed.

I touched her shoulder.

"I don't think it was just about money, Amber. Terrance and Rebecca had slept together in high school. She got pregnant and had an abortion and whoever did it messed her uterus up so she can't have kids. Terrance said he believed she always held him responsible for it since he wasn't trying to be a father at that time. He thought she would get over it, but I guess she never did."

"Terrance told you that?"

I nodded my head.

"Yea, he was my best friend. We shared our past, our secrets, everything. He might not have been the perfect husband, but he was *my* husband."

I felt the tears in my eyes. Amber grabbed my hand into hers.

"Do you think he set this up?"

I shrugged my shoulders. I was just as clueless as she was.

We both watched as the police combed my condo looking everywhere for Terrance or his body.

Portia walked in the room and gave us a funny look. I assumed it was because Amber was still holding my hand.

"Okay, I know we have been through a lot over these past few months, but I am not sleeping with either one of you bitches. I may be a lot of things, but one thing is for sure I am strictly dickly. I don't care what has happened."

I just shook my head and laughed. Portia always thought somebody wanted her ass.

Two weeks later

The police never recovered Terrance's body just a bloody hospital gown that he had on, so we assumed he was dead and that Jason had disposed of the body somewhere no one could find. He was declared legally dead considering he was no longer on the life support machine.

I had to go forward with the plans for his memorial.

I took to the podium proudly wearing the dress Terrance had bought me for our first wedding anniversary. It was a Herve Leger, fitted pink bandage dress and it fit me perfectly since I had lost a considerable amount of weight. Amber and Portia also decided to wear other colors besides black at my request.

I looked out into the sea of faces that came to pay their respect to my husband. I decided to have a memorial instead of a funeral.

Since we had no body there was nothing we could place in a casket. Sitting on a stand at the front of the church was a big picture of Terrance after his college graduation.

I knew Terrance didn't like all the fanfare of Teyah's funeral, and he had told me not to make a big deal over his death, so we kept it small between families only. There weren't any flowers because Terrance didn't like them, so I had them sent to the condo. My living room looked like a miniature flower shop. I looked in the front row at Amber and Portia who both wore solemn expressions on their faces. I knew Terrance's death would affect us all in some way and I wasn't jealous at all of the tears that fell from their face. I still couldn't believe how months ago we were all enemies, but now we all had formed a friendship unlike any other. People from all over had sent their condolences for the things they had heard on the news that we had endured. We were interviewed on Oprah and 20/20 about *"The Arrangement"*. Everyone was intrigued to know that we had to live together under one roof just to get a windfall of money. That was just one clause of the will we couldn't get out of. We still had to move in one house for six months in order to secure any type of money for our children. Even though Terrance was dead he still got his damn wish granted.

We agreed on a six bedroom, 4 bathroom house in the suburbs of Chicago. It wasn't as massive as the house Terrance was going to buy from Mariah Gonzalez, but it was big enough for all of us to live in comfortably. We agreed to let our lives be filmed for a reality show for TV so that we could at least get some money to hold on to. I wasn't sure how living with the other two women would be, but I just had to hope and believe that somehow, someway God would work it out.

Terrance

Somewhere in Paris

"Ellen get out here you are going to want to see this," the man said to his wife.

The fat white woman appeared in the doorway.

"Oh my God in heaven is that who I think it is?" She yelled.

"Yes he has come back to us," the man said.

Ellen ran over to me, falling at my feet and kissing the ground beneath me.

"Sweet Jesus, I can't believe you are alive! I thought we killed you. When Tanya had a funeral for you back in the states, all I kept thinking was we are so screwed."

I sighed at the sound of Tanya's name.

"So the drug worked for you my son?" The man asked while touching my face and arms. "Yes the drug was so potent it almost killed me for real. I think one of my lungs collapsed because I am having trouble breathing," I replied.

Quickly, he ushered me to an exam table and put a gas mask on my face.

"You are definitely on your way to becoming a millionaire. Once we tell people in Hollywood what we did, this drug will fly off the shelves. It will make even the best actor's death scene truly believable."

He smiled and grabbed his stethoscope

"Let's take things one step at a time. I need to check your vitals. Your heart sounds are scratchy, but I'm sure everything will return to normal once the drug wears off."

Ellen and Michael March were scientists I met on a plane while traveling to Paris years ago. Tanya was asleep and we had engaged in a very wonderful conversation. They told me about an experimental drug they were trying to get approved by the FDA to sell to actors in Hollywood for enhanced death scenes. When I told them about my condition and the thing I was trying to do, they more than happily obliged, especially when I paid them fifteen million to do it. They created a drug that would allow me to fake my death. Once the doctor told me I had beaten the stages of lung cancer, but tested positive for HIV, I discharged myself to my home and created my plan. I had to hire a team of nurses and an unsuspecting doctor to follow through with my treatment. Everything had fallen into place like clockwork.

Ellen placed her hands on my face.

"Why didn't you just come out and tell your wife what was going on? I'm sure she would have understood?"

"Understood? Tanya? You think my wife would have liked hearing that her husband was bisexual and had contracted HIV? There is no way I was going to live like that. I have sons. I want them to have a normal life. I don't want them to be ridiculed for the way of life I have chosen. This was the only way I could think of to protect them."

I stopped talking, choking back my tears. "My best friend, Jason is the reason I am in this predicament. He introduced me to this lifestyle becoming my first male experience. I thought it was just something I could chalk up to experiencing in college that would go away, so I slept with as many women as possible to let go of the thoughts. They never went away. He and I were living a lie. There was no way my father would ever accept me, so killing myself off was the best thing to do."

Ellen shook her head.

"I don't understand why you did this. You had enough money to make whatever life you wanted. The settlement was more than enough to move you into another city or state where you would be accepted. What about Tanya and the other women? How do you know they didn't contract HIV from you?"

I shook my head as the tears fell

"I don't expect you to understand why I did what I did. I don't even understand it! I do know for a fact that they are all negative. One of my nurses was able to acquire a blood sample from each of them when I was sick. She told them I needed blood and they gave willingly."

Ellen gave me a pitiful look.

"Well where is this Jason at? Does he know all the trouble you went through to be with him?"

"He's dead. I heard he was killed by the police. What I found out was that he and my attorney had planned to kill me and take my money. Their greed got the best of them."

Michael came back in the room and handed me a drink.

"How did you get away? We saw the news and those police combed every inch of that building looking for you or your body."

"I hid in a garbage compactor until the next morning and then I made my way to a homeless shelter. No one would have ever thought to look there for a multi-millionaire. Once things had died down, I caught a cab to the airport, bought my ticket under my fake name, and caught the first flight out of Chicago."

He shook his head and took a sip from his glass.

"Well I just hope it was worth it. You went through great lengths to create a new life, but I must say one day your lies could come back to haunt you. If Tanya were to ever meet up with you again she could sue you for millions if she ever found out."

I did consider that thought but dismissed it.

"That is why I made sure all of them would be financially set. Since they believe I'm dead I doubt that time will ever come," I replied.

There was an awkward silence

"Well cheers to a new you. What will you name yourself?" Ellen asked.

"I think I like the name Joaquin. It fits me don't you think?"

They smiled at me and we clinked glasses.

I never expected to do the things I did, but it was too late to turn back and Terrance Davenport was now officially dead

Epilogue

Six Months Later

"Which one of you broads used all of my tampons?" Portia screamed at the top of her lungs.

Tanya was sitting in the living room on the couch with her feet underneath her. She stared at the camera guy who had the camera pointed right at her face. She rolled her eyes as she looked to the left. She could see another guy holding the handle of a pole with a big fuzzy thing at the end of it over her head. She assumed it was the microphone that would project the sound of her voice for the millions of viewers watching her life on TV.

She shook her head in disbelief that she agreed to let a film crew follow her every move around the house for three months. Amber tried to stay out of camera view, but as soon as she opened her mouth a camera was shoved in her face.

"Portia, no one uses your tampons but you. If you kept up with your stuff you wouldn't blame us for using your things," Amber said.

Portia came storming into the room. She loved the attention the camera crew gave her and she found a way to get plenty of camera time with her theatrics.

"I am getting sick of living with you two bitches. You sit there perched on that couch all high and mighty judging me as you have always done. Look at my precious son, come here sweetie."

Tanya and Amber looked at each other and frowned. They already knew what was coming next. They watched as Portia grabbed her son TJ who happened to be running by and hugged him. He pushed and pulled away from Portia until she finally released her grasp and let him go.

"I'm getting so sick of her fake made- for- TV attitude like she gives a damn about anyone beside herself," Amber tried to whisper.

The man holding the overhead microphone tried to lower it so he could hear the conversation.

"I heard that white bitch. If you hugged your son more often maybe he wouldn't have to hug on that little boy down the street," Portia fired back.

Amber noticed the producer on her right motioning for her to get up. Following his instructions she got up from the couch and headed to where Portia was standing.

"What the hell did you just say?" Amber asked boldly.

"You heard me. I saw Nathan hugging that little boy down the street. It wasn't a friendly hug either."

The second camera man moved out of the way to allow Tanya enough room to get through without tripping. She got up from the couch to stand in between the two of them.

"Are you saying my son likes boys?"

"Does a bear shit in the woods?"

Portia looked at the camera and smiled. The producer made a cutting motion toward his throat.

"Cut. We are going to have to edit that. Portia, please stop smiling in the camera. That's why we set up the confessional room downstairs for when you want that one on one time to talk to your audience and talk directly into the camera. Right now we want your interactions with each other to look as natural as possible and not so forced," he said.

Tanya laughed.

"There is nothing natural about Portia. All of her actions are forced."

Amber gave Tanya a high five. Portia stuck up her middle finger at both of them.

"Both of you can go to hell. I'm the only real reason the ratings are so high anyway. You two are boring. You eat, clean, sleep and shit. You never have any men around and you are always posted up in front of a TV. Tanya, if you aren't careful you are one cheeseburger away from being fat again."

This time Tanya stepped to Portia. The producer quickly made a motion with his hand to the camera man behind her, and he picked his camera up and followed her.

"You right we are boring. You have all the action going on. You have so many men running through this house I thought I was at Dicks R' Us. For your information your son has been stealing your tampons. If you ever decide to wash your dirty ass laundry you would find the pile of tampons down there that have been constructed into some type of art form," Tanya replied.

Portia stared at Tanya for a second before disappearing into the basement. Another cameraman followed behind her.

"I am truly counting down the days so I can move out," Tanya said to Amber.

"I know what you mean. I have my calendar marked and ready. I plan on bringing in the next month with my new man."

Tanya whipped her head around in Amber's direction.

"What new man?"

"Tony and I decided to make our relationship exclusive now that all the drama is over."

"Shut up! Really? Wow, that is great I'm happy for you girl"

Tanya gave Amber a hug. Amber left the room to check on her son who was upstairs in his room playing video games. She wasn't sure if Portia was just acting for the cameras as normal, or if she really meant she had seen him hugging on a boy. She needed to talk to him about it right away. A camera man followed her as she went upstairs.

There was absolutely no privacy in the house unless they went to the bathroom or had to change their clothes.

Tanya sat in a daze as the camera crew moved around the house. Portia found someone on the phone to cuss out and perform her theatrics for, so their attention had been diverted once again back to her. Tanya stared out the window as she reminisced about the good times with her late husband until a knock at the door interrupted her.

"I got it."

She walked to the door and found a very handsome man wearing a three piece suit at her doorstep. The camera guy was right by her side filming her interaction.

"Are you Mrs. Terrance Davenport?" The man asked.

She paused; the reality of Terrance's death still was hard to swallow.

"I was. How may I help you?"

He extended his hand.

"My name is Jeremiah Freeman I am Terrance Davenport's estate attorney may I come in?"

Tanya looked at him before shaking his hand, and then at the camera guy standing next to her.

"Actually that might not be a good idea." She stepped onto the porch pulling the door away from the camera guy.

"We are filming a reality show and there are cameras everywhere, so unless you want to be on TV I suggest we talk out here."

Jeremiah thought about it for a second before agreeing to stay outside. He passed her an envelope with her name on it.

"What's this?" She asked.

"Your husband asked for this to be delivered six months after you all moved into the house."

"It has only been five so far," she responded.

"I know but you will definitely want to take a look at what's inside."

Tanya gave him a curious look before opening the manila envelope. Inside were open date plane tickets to Jamaica, Paris, London, and St. Tropez, along with a check for 60 million dollars.

"Are you kidding me? I love these places! I thought we had to stay in the house for a full six months before we received any of the settlement money."

"That's just your money. The other women have envelopes that will be given to them. He wanted you to be able to move out first." Tanya put her hand over her mouth. There was a handwritten letter inside. She recognized it as Terrance's handwriting. She pulled it out and read it immediately.

My dearest wife, If you are receiving this letter then you already know I must be gone. I apologize for all the pain you have had to endure over the past few months. I know you are a strong woman and I know God will bless you. Take the money and find a house that you love. Make sure it has a pool you know how you like to swim. Do something you enjoy, or write that cook book you used to talk about back in college. I picked your favorite places to travel to so whenever you are ready just get on a plane and go. The hotels listed on the back of this letter are all inclusive so you won't have to spend a dime of the money I left you. There are no words to express how much pain I feel for the things you have had to endure on my behalf. Just know that I have always loved you and always will. Don't spend all your nights crying over me. Fix your hair up, get your nails done, and buy yourself something nice to wear. There is a handsome eligible bachelor standing in front of you that I know would do right by you. You have my blessings to move on and live your life. I used to think Jason was the man for you but I have a feeling he is dirty so leave him alone. I love you forever and a day, always,

Terrance.

Tanya was in tears after reading the letter. She looked up and found Jeremiah still standing in front of her. This time she took a long hard look at him. He was indeed handsome. He had to be about 6'1 with honey brown skin and cocoa colored eyes. His close cut hair was neat and his suit was tailored made to fit him perfectly. He smiled at her flashing the whitest teeth she had ever seen. She was suddenly aware of her appearance. Tanya was sporting an old gray jogging suit with no shoes on and had her hair in a ponytail.

"I must look a mess," she said consciously touching her hair.

"No you don't. You are beautiful just like he told me you would be."

Tanya smiled for the first time in six months and felt butterflies in her stomach.

"Would you like to have lunch with me sometime?"

"Sure I'd love that," Jeremiah replied.

There was silence between them.

"Well since my job here is done I will let you get back to all those cameras inside. Call me sometime."

He handed her a business card. Tanya smiled and he turned and walked away.

She looked at the check again and did a little dance before turning to walk back inside the house. She entered the foyer and screamed.

"I'm rich bitches and I'm getting the hell out of here!"

Portia and Amber eventually received their envelopes two weeks later and everyone moved out of the house into their own individual homes.

Portia Jackson found a two bedroom condo overlooking the ocean in Florida. She is currently pursuing a career in acting. She landed the role as the leading lady in her first feature film "Hood Girls". Her son TJ lives with his grandparents who moved back to Jamaica and he gets to see his mother every summer.

Amber did bring in the new month with her new boyfriend, Tony Wallace. She finally graduated from college with her business degree and opened up a center for victims of domestic violence with the money she was left. She and her son Nathan still reside in Chicago. She still hasn't spoken to her mother, but she has finally forgiven her for the shooting.

Terrance's parents, Thomas and Nilana Davenport, hold an annual celebration every year in Jamaica in remembrance of their son. Tanya attends every year with her son Ty, her new husband Jeremiah, and her new baby girl Jana. She always gets a funny feeling that Terrance is watching over her and when she sees the strange man standing in the background, she winks at him and smiles.

About the Author

Shay, has been an avid reader and writer since she was a young child. Her first publishing adventure was in 2005 when her short story titled "The Good Ol' Days" was bought and published in the anthology, "Social Security in the hood we take care of our own!"

Shay went on to join the Amiaya Entertainment team and had her first novel "Truth Hurts" published in 2006.

After parting ways with the publisher a year later, Shay didn't stop writing. She went on to contribute to several anthologies:

My Time Publications:

That's the Way Love Goes-(Twisted Love)

A Place to Go (If It Isn't Love)

Take Over Publishing

Street Vices (Imitation of Life)

Shay also ventured out in her writing abilities by becoming a screenwriter. In 2009 she joined a group called Brothas & Sistas After Dark a.k.a BSAD Live:A show featuring improvs,sketches, interviews, & a live discussion based around urban relationships.

Missing the joy of writing books Shay decided to refocus her energy on her first love and decided to self publish her second novel, "THE ARRANGEMENT."

Shay is currently at work on "Truth's revenge" her third novel and the sequel to Truth Hurts. She also is working on a teen series and plans to release many more books in the future.

www.ingramcontent.com/pod-product-compliance
Lightning Source LLC
Chambersburg PA
CBHW071129170626
46809CB00002B/543